The Hungry Wind

Soinbhe Lally

POOLBEG

For my cousins
Maureen, Patricia and Theresa
in Brisbane

Published 1997 by
Poolbeg Press Ltd,
123 Baldoyle Industrial Estate,
Dublin 13, Ireland

Reprinted January 1998
Reprinted August 2000

The moral right of the author has been asserted. A catalogue record for
this book is available from the British Library.

ISBN 1 85371 717 7

Cover illustration by Alison Gault
Cover design by Poolbeg Group Services Ltd
Set by Poolbeg Group Services Ltd in AGaramond 12.5/14
Printed and bound in Great Britain by
Cox & Wyman Ltd, Reading, Berkshire.

About the Author

Soinbhe Lally was born in Enniskillen, Co Fermanagh and went to Queens University, Belfast. Soinbhe lives with her husband and four children in Rossnowlagh, Donegal.

Soinbhe Lally has published numerous short stories, plays and satirical items with various newspapers and journals including *Irish Press* New Writing and *Atlantic Monthly* and has won the Hennessy Literary Award.

Other Poolbeg titles include *Song of the River* and *A Hive for the Honey-Bee*. Soinbhe Lally has retold traditional Irish fairy tales for *The Poolbeg Book of Irish Fairy Stories for Children,* an illustrated picture book, which will be published in 1998.

Praise for **Song of the River**

". . . an unusual and mystical adventure." *Sunday Tribune*

" . . . a book to reach for." *Sunday Tribune*

"The distinctive and appealing personalities of Fingal, Coral Bud, Gaffer and Bubble shine through in the informative and skilfully crafted story of fish and river lore." *The Big Guide to Irish Children's Books*

Praise for **A Hive for the Honey-Bee**

" . . . one of the most original pieces of fiction to have appeared this year." *Children's Books in Ireland*

" . . . positively buzzing with ideas, cleverness and inventiveness . . ." *Children's Books in Ireland*

" . . . a timeless and invaluable joy, a treat for readers of all ages . . ." *Donegal Democrat*

"This story is loud and busy and sweet – an excursion inside a hive of honey-bees." *RTE Guide*

"[A] most original and engaging story." *The Irish Times*

"*Circular from Poor Law Commission calling the attention of the Board of Guardians to the great increase in poverty and distress among the labouring population of the union in consequence of the failure of the potato crop and expressing their earnest wish that . . . the whole accommodation which the workhouse affords will be placed in requisition during a considerable period commencing from the close of the present Autumn.*"

Minutes of Meeting of the Ballyshannon Union Board of Guardians, 12 September 1846

To Each Poor Law Inspector, March 7 1848:

"*The Commissioners for administering the Laws for Relief of the Poor in Ireland forward for your information several copies of a communication . . . on the subject of young persons at present inmates of Irish Workhouses, who may be eligible for emigration to South Australia . . . Your attention is especially called to that part of the letter of the Emigration Commissioners which relates to the peculiar advantage of obtaining young females, eligible and willing to emigrate.*"

One

It was the harvest fair day. Early in the morning Marya and Breege were ready, their long yellow hair combed and neatly plaited. Impatiently they waited while Mama stacked turf on the fire and covered it with ashes to keep the fire in till they came back. Then she sent them to the well for water.

"Oh Mama, can't it do when we come home?" they protested.

"Go and get it now. It will save going later."

They set off along the lane, past the houses and through the potato gardens. Old crazy Siubhan was there on hands and knees, searching through the lazy-beds for any stray potatoes which the harvesters might have missed. When she saw Marya and Breege she knelt upright. "You're for the fair, are you?" she asked. "Mind the trick o' the loop man doesn't run away with one of you."

"Mind he doesn't run away with yourself," Marya retorted.

"Aye, he could do worse." Siubhan cackled with laughter.

Marya and Breege kept to the grassy verge, avoiding the freshly dug earth in the lazy-beds. They were lucky in the lane. Their potatoes did not catch the potato disease which destroyed the crop in other places. Every house had harvested its crop of potatoes and stored them safely in pits for the long winter ahead.

"It's the wind from the sea that keeps the infection away from us," old Peter said wisely. "The sea wind is salty and salt can cure anything, even mackerel."

Dada was already gone with Tom and old Peter to load barrels of salted mackerel into Peter's boat. When Marya and Breege came back from the well Mama was combing Packey's golden curls round her finger, making them hang in ringlets like a girl's. Packey was blessed, Mama said. He was born blessed and could never do wrong in this world. Yet Marya remembered the day Packey was born, how Mama shrieked and wailed when they told her.

But now she didn't seem to mind. Packey was her pet. She let him cling to her petticoat and hide in its folds whenever he was frightened or shy. She carried him in her arms even though he was too big to be carried and dressed him in petticoats at an age when other boys wore breeches. Packey loved to laugh, his mouth gaping and his head lolling, and everyone who heard him laughed too because there was no harm in his laughter.

As soon as he was ready, Marya and Breege each took him by the hand and raced with him to the strand. The boat was ready and the men were waiting. "Up you go," Dada said, lifting Marya and placing her in the prow of the boat. He lifted Breege and Packey and put them beside Marya. They had to wait till Mama and Susan came. Tom ran to meet them. He seized Susan and lifted her up in the air. She squealed with delight.

"Be careful," Mama said indignantly. A little abashed, Tom placed Susan carefully in the boat. Susan and Tom were only a year married. Soon they would have a baby and that, Mama and the other married women agreed, would cure them of being silly.

Tom was Dada's younger brother. He did not have to go far to find his bride. Susan lived right next door with her father, old Peter. It was different when Dada married Mama. She came from the other side of the bay. On the day of their wedding, the boatmen who ferried Dada across the bay had to row all the way, but when they brought Mama home they hoisted a sail and let the boat run before the wind. That was a good omen, Dada said.

Each man took an oar and the boat moved away swiftly from the strand. "Turn her round," Peter called when they drew near to the river channel. He leaned against his oar, holding it as a rudder in the water, while Dada and Tom rowed strongly on the other side. The boat turned sharply, swept through the narrow opening in the river bar and into the estuary.

Soon the town came into view. First the church with its clock tower on top of a green hill, then the town itself, its high rooftops and grey stone walls. The sun burned warmly on Marya's face and the air was humid. "There'll be thunder," old Peter warned. "We'd best not dally too late."

The boat drew near to a stone quay. A hundred yards upriver, white water cascaded among overhanging rocks and crashed into the harbour pool below. "Look, Packey, at the waterfall," Marya said and Packey laughed with delight.

When the boat reached the quay, Tom took a rope and leapt on to the stone steps. Dada kept the boat steady while the women and children climbed out. Then the men unloaded the barrels of mackerel.

A fish buyer who did business on the quay came at once and spoke to Dada in English. "What is he saying?" old Peter asked and frowned when Mama and Susan translated the buyer's offer into Irish. Peter, like all the old people in the lane, spoke only Irish. The younger men and women and the children spoke Irish most of the time but knew enough English to greet a stranger or make a bargain.

Dada refused to sell to the fish buyer at the price he was offering. A sly dirty man with a greasy rag tied on his neck came forward. He forced the lid off one of the barrels and snorted at the smell of mackerel. "Only half salted," he said to the buyer. Marya knew he was lying. She had helped Mama and Susan to salt the mackerel. They used good coarse sea salt and every fish in the cask was laid in a bed of salt.

Dada waved the men away. "There's other agents," he said. Tom put the lid back on the barrel. The buyer named a higher price. Marya could see that he was eager to buy.

"Hold your price," Peter said in Irish. "Let him bid again."

"We'll split the differ," the buyer said.

The sly dirty man seized Dada's hand and slapped his palm on his. "You'll take it, you're a decent man." Dada shook his head. The buyer raised his offer once more. Dada nodded. The buyer spat on his palm and shook hands with Dada. He reached deep into his breeches pocket, took out a fistful of silver coins and counted them into Dada's hand. Dada handed back a luck-penny. The dirty man rolled the barrels along the quay and stacked them alongside other barrels.

Dada gave the money to Peter. Peter counted it out, giving a share to each man, allowing himself an extra share because he owned the boat and nets. He gave Marya, Breege and Packey a penny each. Dada gave most of his share of money to Mama, keeping back only the price of a bag of oatmeal and a shilling for himself.

Two

In the town, the streets were thronged. On all sides rose the squeals and cries of animals. Every year when they came to the harvest fair, Marya wondered how there could be so many people together in one place. Where did they come from? Where did they go when the fair was over?

A drove of geese, herded by small children, cackled and hissed as they passed. A man pushed his way through the crowd, pulling behind him a donkey laden with two creels of apples. "When you hear the church clock strike three it will be time to go home," old Peter said before going off with Dada and Tom. Packey went with Mama and Susan. Marya and Breege went together.

They stopped to watch a man who made pewter plates spin on the end of a stick. He spun two plates on two sticks, tossed the plates in the air and caught them on the tips of the sticks as they came down. Then a boy at a street corner caught their attention. He was singing in a clear voice which rang out above the din of the fair. His song had a sweet slow air which they had never heard before. The boy finished his song and, noticing that they were listening, held up a sheaf of ballads and called out, "A penny a sheet. Only a penny for a new song."

Marya already had the air of the song in her head. She could always learn an air by listening to it once. She wished she could read. If she could read, she would have bought the words of the new song.

They stopped at a stall which was spread with coloured sweets. It took Breege a long time to choose a halfpenny sugar stick. Marya almost bought one too but decided not to spend her penny yet. Some other stall might have something she wanted more.

They went round a corner and down another street. A woman with a basket of coloured ribbons shouted, "Ribbons and lace, take your pick." Breege touched one ribbon and then another, trying to choose between them. "What do you think?" she asked, holding a red satin ribbon against her hair.

"That's your colour," the woman said.

"It really does suit you," Marya agreed.

Breege bought the ribbon for a halfpenny. She unplaited her hair from its neat braids and tied it loosely with the ribbon. She looked so pretty and grown up that Marya decided to buy a ribbon too. She could buy a ribbon and still have a halfpenny left.

Just as she reached into the basket someone tugged her sleeve. A woman with a child in her arms asked, "A penny, God bless you, can you spare a penny?"

Marya felt her face go red. She knew she should turn away and ignore the woman. Dada had warned against tricksters and professional beggars who came to fairs to cheat people out of their money. But this woman did not look as if she was lying. She was gaunt and ragged. Two half-naked children clung to her petticoat. Marya thrust her penny towards her and turned quickly away, ashamed of her misgivings.

The excitement of the fair suddenly palled. It was not just that she had no money to spend. She was suddenly aware of other ragged people, men, women and children, with hunger written in their pinched faces. Some tried to beg. Others crouched in corners or leaned against walls, too exhausted to call out to passers-by. They must be the people they had heard about, the hungry people whose potatoes had wilted and died in the fields. She could see them now on all sides, people with sunken eyes staring emptily at those who were not hungry.

She felt stifled. The crush of the crowd and the smells of the fair made her head ache. "Let's go back to the quay," she said to Breege.

In the lane which led to the harbour, tall warehouses cast a cool shade. Marya felt better there. They passed between lines of carts stacked high with sacks of oats, waiting their turn to be weighed before being unloaded. So much food yet people were hungry. Marya thought of the barrel of mackerel at home which Dada had set aside for their own use, and their store of potatoes in the potato pit. If anyone was hungry in the lane, Dada and Mama would share with them. Perhaps the merchants of the town would take pity on the hungry people in their streets and share their stores of food with them.

She sat with Breege on a grassy knoll above the harbour. The sky was dark and low. They watched a sailing ship on the other side of the harbour pump filthy bilge-water into the river. She was the *Charlotte* from Nova Scotia, one of the Canadian timber boats. Dada knew all the ships, their names and where they came from.

They sat for a long time. Above the roar of the falls, they heard the church clock strike each of the quarter hours between two and three. At last it struck three. Mama and Susan were first to arrive, leading Packey between them. Packey was sticky-faced and sucking a sugar stick. They sat with Marya and Breege on the grassy knoll. Eventually the men arrived, their cheeks flushed and their eyes bright.

"Isn't it a shame?" Susan said to Mama. "You let men out of your sight and they're away to fill themselves with porter."

"It's a disgrace," Mama agreed. Dada put down the sack of oatmeal which he was carrying on his shoulder and grinned widely. One side of his head was dusty with meal.

"Are they fit to row or will the women have to row the boat home?" Susan asked. Tom caught her in a wild embrace before she could say any more. Laughing, she pushed him away.

"Come on, the lot of you. Get into the boat or are you going home at all today?" old Peter said crossly. Susan laughed even more. Old Peter was famous for the way a pint of porter made him cantankerous.

"All right," she said, still giggling as Tom insisted on leading her down the stone steps and lifting her into the boat.

They cast off and moved quickly downstream, carried by the river current. Marya felt tired and vaguely oppressed. Her head still ached. She cooled her hand in the river water and wiped her face with it. As they crossed the bar, the sky lit up with a silent flash of light.

"There's weather yonder," old Peter said and he pulled more strongly on his oar.

When they landed, Marya and Breege carried bundles and packages for Mama and Susan. Dada heaved the bag of oatmeal on his shoulder and led the way through the dunes. As they drew near the lane they noticed a strange smell, a smell of something rank and putrid. Old Siubhan came running to meet them, her white hair askew. "The potatoes," she cried. "Smell the potatoes."

Dada dropped the sack of meal and started to run. Tom followed. Peter stooped to pick up the bag of meal and hurried after. "What's the matter?" Susan asked anxiously. Nobody answered.

The smell grew stronger as they came close to the lane. Dada was already in the potato garden pulling away the sods and straw which covered his potato pit. He reached into the pit and pulled out a mass of grey slime. Frantically he dug with his two hands. The potatoes he took from the pit were black and rotten.

All evening men and women dug through the potato pits, trying to find some potatoes to save. Thunder crashed overhead and the storm broke. Rain poured down, filling the opened pits with water. Families coming late from the fair screamed in terror when they discovered that their winter store was rotting in the ground. Long after darkness fell Marya could hear the sounds of digging as people tried to find something to save.

Mama brought Susan to sit with her by the fire. Susan sat hunched, shuddering at each lightning flash. "What curse is on us?" she whispered over and over.

Mama took potatoes from the small store in the corner of the house and baked them in the fire. The children ate hungrily but Susan refused to eat. At last Dada and Tom came in. They were tired and dirty. In silence they sat down and ate the potatoes which Mama set before them.

Three

At first there was still money. Dada and Mama had a store of silver coins saved from the summer fishing. If they used it carefully, it would tide them over till the herring season. Peter took money from the long stocking which he kept hidden behind a stone in his chimney and lent it to families who had nothing. They would pay it back when the herring came.

Each day the women and girls went to the rocks to gather seaweed and shellfish. At one end of the strand there were stretches of muddy sand encrusted with acres of mussels but they were not allowed to pick those. For fear that hunger would tempt them the landlord's agent, Mister Hamilton, sent his men to warn tenants that the mussel beds were not included in their shore rights. The agent lived in a tall stone house a mile away from the lane. When mussels were in season, a boy was sent from the tall house to gather them for his master's table.

"That they may choke him," old Peter said bitterly. "I remember when Alexander Hamilton had only a thatch over his head. Put a beggar on horseback and he'll ride to hell."

Several times each day the fishermen went to the top of the headland to watch for signs of herring. The days grew short and the weather cold but the herring did not come. Sometimes they fished with lines, but it was not the season for line fishing and they caught little.

"I can sell the boat and nets," Peter said when the meal bin was almost empty and there was no money left in the long stocking.

"No, you must keep them, the herring might come yet," Dada said. He went to the town and pawned his boots. When he arrived home barefoot he was carrying only a half-stone bag of meal. "They're charging twice the price for meal," he said bitterly. "I gave three shillings and four pence for this."

It was rumoured that the merchants were hoarding meal, waiting for prices to go higher. Then came news of a government roadworks scheme which would give employment to the poor. "Why would anybody make a road on the top of the cliff, a road that goes nowhere?" people wondered.

Nobody could answer that but Dada said there must be a reason, and if it gave work to people in a hard time, there must be some good in it. In November the relief works began. There were wages of a pound of yellow meal a day and a shilling each week. Tom said he could wait for herring no longer; Susan was growing pale and thin. Dada agreed and together they went to the relief works.

A pound of yellow meal a day was not enough to feed a family and the promised wages were not always paid but Dada and Tom still went to work because a pound of meal and the promise of a shilling were better than nothing. Gale day came and rents were due but nobody in the lane had money to pay.

"They've often waited for the rent before," old Peter said. "I don't suppose they'll be hard on us in these hungry times."

The winter frost came early and the ground froze hard. It was too cold for Mama to bring Packey to the shore. Breege stayed at home to mind him while Marya went with Mama. Down on the rocks, the air was bitterly cold. Waves crashed and swept back with a sucking sound.

Marya searched in crevices and under ledges in rock pools but she still had only a small bundle of carrageen moss when daylight began to fade. She groped under clump after clump of seaweed searching for winkles and whelks. The white whelks were easier to see in the gathering darkness. Their meat was tough and indigestible but they would have to do.

Dark shapes moved about on the rocks, other women and girls searching and gathering. One of them straightened up, a black figure against the white of breaking waves. "Marya, it's time to go home." It was Mama's voice.

Marya was glad to tie up her bundle. They climbed over a wall of boulders beside the stream and followed a path bordered by willows. Frozen grass crackled under their bare feet. The wet bundles dripped against their petticoats, soaking through the coarse flannel.

In the lane the houses were a huddle of dark shapes. The doors were already closed. Only the light of turf fires showed in chinks between door boards. Smoke rose in pale ghostly spirals into the night, smelling of warmth and home.

Packey ran out to meet them. "Look, look," he shouted excitedly, pointing at the starry sky. Mama took him by the hand and led him inside. The house was lit by the red glow of the fire. In the semi-darkness Marya could see Breege placing sods of turf under a simmering pot.

They emptied their harvest of shellfish and seaweed on to the table. Mama set aside half of what they had gathered. "Take these to Susan," she said to Marya.

"Bless you. There's the makings of a good

soup in this," Susan said, opening the bundle which Marya brought.

She went to a corner, lifted a brown pitcher from the floor and poured milk into an earthen jug. Marya watched, wide-eyed. No one in the lane owned a cow. "Where did you get it?" she asked.

"Tom milked one of Alexander Hamilton's cows," Susan said softly and placed a finger on her lips. Marya was shocked. It was wrong to steal. She hid the jug in a fold of her petticoat and carried it home.

Limpets were already sizzling in the hot ashes at the edge of the fire, making a mouthwatering smell. Mama took them from their shells and dropped them into the soup. She added carrageen and yellow meal.

"You stir it, Marya," she said, putting the long pot stick into Marya's hand. The heat of the fire made steam rise from her damp petticoat as she stirred. When the soup was ready, Mama poured it into noggins. Packey smacked eagerly.

"Careful, you'll burn your mouth," Breege said, taking the wooden cup away from him. Packey laughed excitedly and waited.

Mama set the pot at the side of the fire with Dada's portion. Dada was gone since early morning. He had not come home yet even though the ground was frozen too hard for men to work at road-making. That morning Mama had fretted when she heard Dada coughing. "It's only a cold, I'll be all right," Dada insisted and he went to work.

It was late when he came home. He was shivering with cold. He went directly to the fire and sat with his bare feet in the ashes, rubbing his hands and arms to warm them. From time to time he was racked by coughing.

"Hush, children," Mama said and coaxed Packey to lie on the pallet of straw in the corner which he shared for a bed with Marya and Breege. Dada shook his head when she offered him his share of soup and stayed by the fire, his head between his hands.

In the morning Marya woke early. She was as hungry as if she had eaten nothing the night before. She heard Dada moving about the dark kitchen. "You're sick," Mama said. "Stay at home for the one day. You'll get your death going out in this cold."

"There might be work today. They'll be giving out meal even if there's no work." Marya heard the sound of the latch and felt the icy draught from the doorway as the door opened and closed.

"If he had his boots itself," Mama murmured anxiously. She leaned over the ashes of the fire, blowing the live embers till they glowed red.

Marya stayed in bed, with Breege and Packey curled up on each side, till daylight seeped under the door. Packey was first to get up. "Out, out," he demanded and Marya got up to take him outside. Feathery flakes of snow drifted in the air. Packey raced up and down on the frozen ground in front of the house cheering with excitement.

For breakfast they ate a thin gruel made with the last of the meal. "If that doesn't fill you, you can eat shore meat," Mama said, putting a small heap of cooked whelks and winkles on the table. Marya picked a winkle from a shell and ate it. It made her stomach feel queasy. Usually she liked the salty taste of the small sea snails, but they'd eaten winkles every day this week. She would have to wait till she was hungrier before she could eat any more.

All morning the snow fell. The wind whistled in the chimney and under the door. Marya and Breege sat by the fire plaiting bent-grass for Mama to weave into mats. The bent-grass grew in the sand-dunes. It was tough and wiry and could be plaited and woven. Already Mama had been twice to the town, knocking at doors of well-to-do houses. Her mats were neatly made and she earned enough to buy a little extra meal.

While she wove, she sang a sad song of love and heartbreak and the girls sang with her, copying the turns and inflections of the music. Mama was a famous singer, not just in the lane but in the surrounding townlands. Before the potatoes rotted, when there was still singing and dancing, Mama was always asked to sing because of her sweet voice and for the way she gave every air a new turn each time she sang.

Night was falling when the men came. They carried Dada between them. His body was cold and stiff. One of the men placed a small bundle of meal and a silver shilling on the table. At first Mama did not speak. She touched Dada's face, shaking her head in disbelief. Then she fell to her knees. Packey clung to her and screamed in terror as she raised her voice in the lament for the dead.

At first Marya could not cry. She hid her face in her hands, refusing to look. It was not possible. Dada, so big and strong, so full of life, he could not be dead. When Peter and Tom brought a door from another house and laid Dada's corpse on it she shuddered at the sounds they made. Then somebody brought a candle. Its flickering light shone on Dada's pale face and she knew then that he was really dead. Terrible sobs racked her. Susan put her arms round her and led her to the fireside to sit with Mama.

Four

The night was long. Neighbours came in twos and threes till the kitchen was filled with people. They stroked the children's heads and whispered blessings over them. Marya meant to stay awake all night with Mama and the other women, but some time before morning she woke up and found herself curled on the pallet alongside Packey and Breege. She remembered with a terrible convulsion of grief that Dada was dead.

The kitchen was almost dark except for a stump of candle which guttered beside the corpse. The fire burned low in the hearth. Mama and Susan crouched beside it without moving or speaking. Other women made a line of dark shadows on the bench by the back wall.

The men were gathered in the corner by the door. They were deep in conversation and from time to time a voice was raised and other men hushed the speaker. "She's got a full cargo of bacon," Tom whispered. His voice was easy to recognise.

"Shipping food out of the harbour and the people left to starve," said another voice bitterly.

Marya knew what they were talking about. Everybody knew. A schooner was lying off the river bar, waiting for a pilot to take it up the river. All week there were rumours that the merchants in the town, fearful that the hungry people would riot and rob the warehouses, were preparing to ship out their stores of food.

At first nobody believed the rumours. Surely the authorities would not allow it. But now a ship was lying off the river bar. A cargo ship, floating high, with ballast in her hold. There was only one cargo in the town, the stores of oatmeal and bacon which landlords and their agents had extorted from the hungry people.

"They'll take her up on the morning tide," Tom said. "It'll take two days to load her."

"They might wait longer for a wind."

A voice asked. "Are you in?"

"I am." Marya recognised old Peter's voice. "You can count on me and my boat."

When it was light, Mama gave Dada's shilling wages to one of the neighbour women. "Go to the priest. Ask him to bless some earth and some holy water."

"I'll take Marya with me," the woman said. "Maybe he'll not take the money when he sees that you have children."

Soinbhe Lally

Marya would have preferred not to go. The thought of leaving the house while Dada was lying there filled her with misery. However she did not argue. She let the woman wrap her feet in rags and followed her blindly through the snow. It was only three miles to town but now it felt like a hundred miles. Her feet ached with cold and the frozen hem of her petticoat rubbed painfully against her legs.

They waited at the priest's door while a man-servant went to tell the priest what they wanted. A smell of frying bacon came from inside the house. The man-servant returned. "Have you brought the earth?"

"Can I speak to His Reverence?" the woman asked.

"No, you can't. He's having his breakfast."

The woman handed over a cloth filled with earth and an empty noggin. The man-servant waited expectantly. "This child has lost her father. She has a brother and a sister. Their poor mother has nothing but this shilling."

The manservant looked contemptuously at the woman and then at Marya. "Do you want a blessing or don't you?"

"Give him the shilling," Marya whispered, terrified that he would refuse them.

The man went back inside and reappeared a few minutes later carrying the bundle of earth and the noggin which was now filled with blessed water. They trudged home. Marya's mind was numb. She hardly felt the cold any more. It was as if she were walking in a dream, some terrible nightmare from which she could not make herself waken.

"Musha, you're perished," the old women exclaimed when they come through the door. They seized eagerly on the noggin of holy water and the bundle of blessed earth and placed them on a shelf above the fire. Then they gathered round Marya, chafing her hands and unwinding the wet rags from her feet.

"The priest's man took the shilling," she said wearily.

"Don't mind," Mama said. "You got the blessed earth and holy water. That's all that matters."

"That's not what I meant." Marya's lips quivered and she began to cry.

"It's all right." Mama took her hand in her own to chafe it warm. "It's all right," she repeated, understanding the thoughts which Marya could not speak.

All evening and into the night the sound of sawing and hammering echoed in the lane. Somehow old Peter had obtained boards and nails to make a coffin. Susan made gruel. "Eat it. You must eat," she insisted when Mama refused it. Marya realised how hungry she was and ate her share eagerly. She fell asleep at the hearth, curled up beside Mama's feet.

In the morning the snow had turned to sleet and rain. Water dripped from the leaky places in the thatch and the fire made steam rise from the damp earthen floor.

The men went away with shovels to dig the grave. When they came back they brought the coffin from Peter's house. It was roughly made of old weathered timber. Peter recited prayers and sprinkled the holy water. Then the lid of the coffin was nailed down. The men carried it outside and four of them heaved it up on their shoulders. They walked slowly along the lane. Marya and Breege walked behind Mama and Packey, splashing through slush and mud.

As they reached the end of the lane, old Siubhan started from her cabin and ran alongside the coffin. "The young are going before the old," she screeched. "Wouldn't you think they would wait their turn?" Some of the women hushed her and let her walk along with them.

In the graveyard there was the smell of freshly-dug earth. Marya cried softly as the men lowered the coffin into the deep hole. Tom sprinkled the blessed earth on the coffin. Then there was a murmur of prayers and a scrape of shovels. Clay thudded on wood with a hollow sound. Breege sobbed loudly. Marya put her arms round her and let her hide her face in her shoulder.

They walked home in silence. The house was cold. Mama sat and stared at the grey ashes of the fire. Neighbour women came to sit with her. Susan stirred the ashes and made the fire blaze up. She ladled water into a small pot and hung it on a hook above the fire. The women keened softly, their voices rising and falling.

"God help the children," moaned one.

Mama turned sharply. "God will only help if we help ourselves."

"But what can you do?"

"I can go to the relief works and ask for my husband's place."

"You cannot work like a man."

"I can dig. I have dug since I was old enough to. And I can carry stones. I will take his place." She looked into the fire and did not speak again. One by one the women went away. Susan left but reappeared in a short while with a noggin of milk and small portion of meal tied in a cloth. "I wish it was more," she said.

"Thank you," Mama murmured and then sat silent again. Breege lifted the pot from the fire and carefully poured in the meal, stirring all the while. She added a pinch of salt and hung the pot over the fire again. The yellow gruel bubbled gently. When it was ready she added the milk and poured it into noggins. Packey ate his up quickly and looked round hopefully for more. Mama let him have hers.

Five

That night Marya slept uneasily. Hunger disturbed her sleep and early in the morning she started awake at the sound of Mama moving about the kitchen. Mama heard her stir. "Breege, are you awake?"

"She's still asleep."

"Marya, you and Breege, mind Packey till I come back."

"Where are you going?"

"To the roadworks."

She slipped away, closing the door quietly behind her. Marya lay awake for a long time before getting up. How could Mama do a man's work? she thought anxiously. What if she became sick too, like Dada? What then? She pushed the thoughts from her mind and tried instead to plan the day ahead. She would have to do Mama's work now. She would go to the rocks and see what food she could find there. Then she would cut bent-grass in the dunes and plait it, ready for making mats.

Packey cried for Mama when he wakened. Marya put her arms round him and rocked him to and fro, the way Mama did, till his sobs subsided. Then Breege began to cry and she had to put her arms round her too.

Susan brought them milk for breakfast. Later, when the tide ebbed, Susan minded Packey while Marya and Breege went to the rocks. There was not much to be found. Some limpets, a red crab which the tide had stranded in a rock pool and some seaweed. When Mama came home she brought a ration of meal.

Susan came from next door. "Did they let you work?"

"They did."

"What are they giving you?"

"They're paying women three farthings a day for carrying stones, and a pound of meal. It will keep us from hunger." She sat down wearily and let Marya and Breege prepare the meal while Packey sat at her feet. He rested his head against her knee and she stroked it. Marya felt a terrible sense of emptiness. Mama was home and still the house seemed empty. It would always feel empty, she thought, without Dada.

Mama went every day to the roadworks. Her hands were blistered and her shoulders ached.

Susan brought salt for her to rub into her hands to harden them.

"Can Marya and Breege come next door?" she asked. "Tom needs a hand with something." Mama did not ask why Tom wanted them. Perhaps she was too tired, Marya thought. She wondered what Tom could want so late in the evening.

They went into the house next door and Marya cried out in fright. Half a dozen black-faced men stood about in the firelight. Breege jumped when one of the men put his face close to hers.

"Don't you know your uncle, girl?"

"Tom?"

One by one they recognised them. Tom, old Peter, John Joe from the other end of the lane. Their faces were blackened with soot. Several women were also in the house. Tom rubbed his hands on the chimney brace and gave his face a final coating of soot. He grinned at Marya and rolled his eyes. His teeth and eyes were fearsomely white.

"What are you doing?" she asked.

"We're going to get our Christmas dinner." He took the pot stick from the hearth and drew on the clay floor. "Now here is the plan, The ship is lying inside the bar, right here. We'll row upriver to the salt works, then downstream again. I'll call out and ask for a light for my pipe. They'll think we're down from the salt works getting saltwater. When I go on board, the rest of you follow."

"Call no man by his name," Peter warned, "it might give him away."

"Marya and Breege, you go with the rest of the women to the black rock on the strand. Wait there till we come. You, Susan, stay here. Keep a lookout."

Tom opened the door and, one by one, the men disappeared into the darkness. The women waited till Susan said it was time to go. Marya and Breege went with them across the fields to the sand-dunes. They followed rabbit pads, avoiding clumps of sharp marram grass. The swish of waves could be heard from the strand and, blacker than the blackness of the night, the black rock loomed against the white water of the river bar.

They could see the dark shape of the schooner and its tall masts up the river. A single lantern was the only sign of life on board. Marya's heart thudded painfully. What if the men were overpowered by the ship's crew? What if the crew had guns? As if in answer to her fears, the report of a pistol shot echoed and re-echoed in the night. A woman whispered a prayer. There were cries and shouts from the ship, then only the suck and surge of the tide on the strand and the crash of waves on the river bar.

It seemed an eternity till they heard a sound, the distant splash of an oar, so faint that Marya could not be sure that she heard it at all. Then another splash, closer this time and, in a few minutes, the dark shadow of Peter's boat as it swept clear of the river bar and across to the strand.

Before the keel crunched on to the sand the women were wading into the water, already unloading sacks and hogsheads of bacon. Marya and Breege took a sack between them and dragged it into the dunes to the wide shallow hole which the men had dug earlier in the day. Then they ran back to the boat for another sack.

They worked swiftly and silently till the boat was emptied and the stolen food, all but one sack of meal and two kegs of lard, stowed in the hole. The men covered it up with sand and laid cut sods of grass on top, treading them carefully to conceal signs of disturbance. They carried the boat up the shore and left it upside-down among other fishing boats. The women brushed the sand with clumps of marram grass to remove telltale footprints.

Tom put the bag of oatmeal on his shoulders and led the way through the dunes. Another man carried the kegs of lard. At the top of a high ridge they stopped to look upriver. Far upstream, lights were moving to and fro.

Tom chuckled. "They think we've gone upstream. They're looking for us there."

"Come on," Peter said, hurrying forward, "the sooner we're home the safer it will be for all of us."

They moved silently among the houses in the lane. A dog barked far off in the distance but nothing else disturbed the stillness. Most of the cabins were completely dark, not even a chink of light showing.

As soon as they were inside, Tom opened the bag of oatmeal and poured a share for each household into the women's aprons. Marya and Breege lifted their petticoats by the hems and let Tom pour meal into them. The kegs of lard were broken open and a large lump of lard put on top of each share of oatmeal.

"I make it three hogsheads of bacon that we've got and two more kegs of lard. It's a pity she wasn't carrying more meal. We got ten bags in the ship's own stores. That leaves nine still in the dunes." Tom looked round. The men nodded in agreement. "We'll take out food only as we need it. That way, no one runs the risk of having it found in their house."

"Let nobody speak a word of this to anyone," Peter added. "The food cannot be shared outside our own households. Otherwise, word will get out."

"Was anybody hurt?" a woman asked. "Who fired the shot?"

"The captain woke up but Tom took the gun away from him," a man said.

"Whisht," Peter said sharply. "Don't tell that story anywhere. Not a word." He glared round fiercely.

The danger was far from over, Marya realised. Women would want to share food with relatives who were hungry too. Men might want to boast about their share in the night's adventure. It would not be easy for the secret to be kept.

She went home with Breege. Their petticoats bulged with their share of oatmeal. "Where did you get it?" Mama asked in astonishment.

Marya looked at Breege but Breege looked away. Marya felt angry. What if the meal *was* stolen? They had a right to it. Why shouldn't they steal if they were hungry? "It's from the ship inside the bar," she said defiantly.

Mama rose silently and held the empty meal bag open. Breege and Marya emptied their petticoats into it. She set the bag carefully into a wooden keg and covered it to keep it safe from mice. Then she sat by the fire and did not speak.

Marya couldn't bear her silence. "I don't care if it's stealing," she said angrily. "We have a right to steal when we're starving."

She fell silent. Mama's shoulders were

quivering and her breath came in quick gasps. She was crying. Marya stood helpless, not knowing what to do.

"We'll make porridge for you, Mama," Brid said quietly. She lifted the pot from the hob and put it over the fire.

Marya helped. She put water in the pot and stirred while Breege poured in the oatmeal. By the time it was ready Mama had stopped crying. She wiped her eyes with the corner of her apron. "Here, Mama, take this," Marya said, offering her a noggin of porridge and a spoon.

Breege poured out porridge for herself and Marya. Packey was asleep. He could have his in the morning. "God forgive us," Mama said in a low voice. Then she started to eat.

For days it was a feast. There was oatmeal porridge three times a day and gruel for supper. The oatmeal porridge tasted delicious after weeks of eating nothing but sour yellow meal. The comfort of a full stomach took the edge off the biting cold and made it easy to forget that one day the hoard of stolen food would run out and they would be hungry again.

Mama continued to go to the works each day and stored the farthings which she earned under a loose stone in the hearth. Her daily ration of yellow meal was added to the oatmeal porridge to make it go further. Some nights there was a light knock on the door. Tom would come in and Mama would hold out the empty meal bag to receive the family's share of oatmeal. On Christmas Eve, he brought a large piece of bacon.

"Bacon for the Christmas dinner," he said, showing the bacon to Packey. Packey sniffed it and laughed excitedly. "Cook it right away," Tom said to Mama, "it wouldn't do to have the smell of bacon about the place in the daytime."

Mama put the bacon into the pot and hung it over the fire. They went to bed. Marya lay thinking of other Christmases when Dada was still with them. Her loneliness became a tight pain in her chest. For a long time she stayed awake, stifling her sobs for fear that Mama would hear.

Six

On New Year's day the landlord's agent sent two of his men to nail a notice to the door of each house.

"What does it say?" Mama asked one of the men but he ignored her question.

Old Siubhan's house was last. She did not make an appearance till the men fixed the notice and turned away. Then she flung open her door. "Tell Alexander Hamilton to keep his paper," she screamed, tearing the notice down and flinging it after them. They paid no attention to her as she followed them along the lane screeching insults and curses.

Nobody in the lane could read the notices. Marya was sent to the next townland to fetch a hedge-schoolmaster who knew how to read. The master was a pale thin man dressed in the shabby remains of a black suit. He placed brass-rimmed spectacles on his nose and peered at one of the notices.

"Well?" Peter demanded.

"It's an eviction notice."

"When?"

"On the last day of the month."

A thin wail arose from the women. Their rents were not paid. But how could they pay rent when there were no potatoes and no herring? Didn't the agent know they would pay when they could?

"It's the burden of the rates," the schoolmaster explained. "The landlords have to pay for the upkeep of the workhouse. If they level a house, they don't have to pay rates for it."

For days the neighbours came and went to each other's houses discussing possible solutions. Some went to the town and asked about passage to England or Glasgow. Others made more ambitious plans. A shipping agent in the town was offering cheap passage to Quebec on ships which carried timber from Canada. If a family could raise enough to send one person, others could follow.

They inspected their possessions. Some had more than others. Peter had a boat and net. It would raise enough to take him and Susan and Tom to America. Once there, they could send back passage-money for Mama and the children.

"Would they let Packey into America?" Mama asked but nobody answered her question.

For those who had nothing to sell there was only one place left to go but nobody spoke of it. Marya had often seen the workhouse in the town, a massive stone building with high walls and iron gates. A place where families were not allowed to be together.

They heard a rumour which diverted their thoughts from eviction. The merchants were offering £20 reward for information which would lead to the apprehension of the gang who carried out an act of piracy and robbed their ship of food. "Imagine," Peter said, rubbing his nose and looking roguish, "a man could be worth £20 if he knew where to find that gang."

For a few hours, people enjoyed the importance of being worth £20. Tom carried a hogshead of bacon from the hoard in the dunes and cut it into portions for each household in celebration of the news. It was the last of the bacon. Until eviction day there would be only oatmeal.

The January spring tide ebbed further than at any other time of the year. Marya and Breege were able to paddle out to offshore rocks where green-brown sloke grew thickly. Back home, they boiled the seaweed in the pot till it turned into black jelly. When the jelly cooled they let Packey help them pat it into cakes which they rolled in oatmeal. Marya greased the griddle with a small piece of bacon fat and let the cakes fry slowly.

A voice at the door made her start. "God bless you, can you spare a bit for the hungry?" it whined. She turned and saw a grey-faced man. Beside him was a thin woman who carried a child in her arms.

Marya wished she had closed the door. Mama had warned them not to let strangers into the house. "Don't come in," she said nervously. "Stay where you are. We'll give you a bit at the door. Mama said to let no one in."

"Is your mother not here?" the man asked, stepping forward.

"She's in my uncle's house next door," Marya said sharply. She rose from the hearth and half-closed the door.

The man stepped back and waited till Breege placed three of the fried sloke cakes on the ground outside the door. He ate two cakes greedily. The woman took the third and tried to feed a piece of it to the child. The child whimpered but did not eat.

"Is it far to the workhouse?" the woman asked.

"The town is three miles away."

"Have you another bit to spare?" the man asked and added slyly, "There's not many can cook with bacon fat in these hard times."

Breege placed another cake on the ground. Then Marya closed the door. "We should have refused them," Breege said.

"No, we could not have turned them away hungry."

Early next morning a hammering at the door startled them awake.

"Who is it?" Mama called out.

"Open in the name of the law," a voice commanded. At the same instant the door burst open and black-coated policemen rushed into the house. Marya and Breege pulled on their petticoats while the men searched the small room, overturning the meal keg to see if anything was concealed in it.

A man snatched Packey by the arm and dragged him outside. "Where is the bacon?" he shouted. Packey screamed in terror.

"Leave him alone," Mama pleaded, following them outside, "he's a poor harmless creature."

"Let him go," said an officer on horseback.

The policeman let Packey go. Packey ran to hide his face in Mama's petticoat. Marya and Breege stood close to her and watched while policemen climbed on the roof. They prodded the thatch with sticks and poles, careless of the damage they were doing. Inside the house there was a loud crash as someone overturned the straw pallet where they slept.

"What's going on here?" said an angry voice. Tom shouldered his way through the onlookers.

"We have a warrant," said the man on horseback, "issued on sworn evidence."

"Whose evidence?"

"His."

The police officer pointed at a ragged man who stood between two policemen. Marya recognised the grey-faced man who had begged at their door the previous day. The police officer dismounted from his horse. He bent down and spoke kindly to Packey.

"There's nothing to be afraid of," he said coaxingly. "You like bacon, don't you?"

Packey turned his head cautiously and, seeing a friendly face, nodded.

"You liked having bacon for dinner?"

Packey nodded vigorously.

"Who gave you the bacon?"

There was a hush. Packey scanned the faces of the onlookers. With a delighted smile, he pointed at Tom. "Arrest him," said the officer.

Tom was seized by several policemen and thrown to the ground. Quickly he was bound and dragged to the road. Susan screamed and tried to follow but Mama held her and led her back into her own house.

Seven

All morning the policemen searched houses. Thatches were broken, bedding overturned. They found nothing. By midday, they gave up. The officer on horseback ordered them together and they marched away. Next morning old Peter went to the town and came back with news that Tom had been arraigned for robbery and sent to the county jail to await trial.

A deep gloom settled over the lane. Marya and Breege harvested endlessly on the seashore. There was little left there now; there were too many people searching the shore for food. Everybody was hungry but nobody dared go to the hoard in the dunes for fear of watchers. Mama took her store of farthings from under the loose stone in the hearth and sent Peter to the town to buy a few pounds of meal so that Susan would not go hungry.

On the day of Tom's trial, Peter set off in the darkness of early morning to tramp fifteen miles to the assizes. The day passed and night fell without any sign of him. One by one neighbours came and sat with Susan, waiting for his return. Marya was nodding and almost asleep when the door opened and Peter came in. He looked tired and dejected. Neighbours stood aside to let him go to his stool at the fireside. He sat down and did not speak.

"Well?" Susan asked.

"He was found guilty."

"What will they do to him?"

"He is sentenced to seven years' transportation."

"Transportation?"

"They will send him to Australia."

Susan sobbed wildly. "I'll never see him again," she wept. "Nobody ever comes back from Australia."

The women wailed, their voices rising and falling as if they were lamenting the dead. Marya shivered. They were mourning for Tom as if he were already dead.

During the days which followed, people sold their possessions for whatever they could raise on them. "The ship-owners will provide food and fresh water for the voyage," they said, "All we need is the passage-money. The shipping agent says there will be work for everybody in America, and free land for anyone who wants it."

Susan did not join in the preparations. She withdrew further into herself with each passing day. There was little to eat but even that little she barely touched. "You must eat," Mama coaxed, trying to make her take some gruel. "Think of the baby. It will not be long now." Susan shook her head and pushed the gruel away.

A letter came. It was the first time a letter came for anybody in the lane. The man who brought it said it was for Susan. "Go, Marya, ask the schoolmaster to come here," Peter said.

Marya went quickly across the fields to the next townland. The door to the master's house was closed. She knocked but nobody came.

"The master's not here any more," said a thin red-haired boy who sat in the open doorway of the next house. "He's gone away to America. Did you want him to read something?"

"He's wanted to read a letter."

"Then it's the truth that you're all ignorant illiterates over in the lane?"

Marya flushed indignantly. "What is it to you?"

"I can read."

She looked at him doubtfully. The boy was only as old as herself. And just as ragged. "What can you read?"

"I can read books. And letters. Did you bring the letter with you?"

"I did not. It's not my letter."

"Well, then, you'd better bring me to the letter if you want it read."

He followed Marya across the fields to the track which led to the lane. "What's your name?" he asked.

"Marya."

"I'm Seamus."

They reached the lane and Marya brought Seamus to Peter's house. "The master's gone to America," she explained. She pointed at Seamus. "He says he can read."

"So I can. If you show me the letter I'll read it, unless it's written in some language I don't know."

"What languages do you know?" old Peter asked suspiciously.

"Irish, English, Latin, Greek and a little French. I lived beside the master, in the next house. He was always teaching us."

Susan handed the letter to the boy. He looked it over quickly. "It's in English but I can give you the meaning in Irish."

Susan nodded.

"It's from your husband Tom. He's on board a convict hulk in the cove of Cork. The ship's surgeon is writing this letter for him. They will not sail for another month. You will be allowed passage to Australia on a female convict ship if you come to Queenstown before it sails."

"Where is Queenstown?"

"In Cork."

"Is it far?"

"Yes, it's a long way."

Susan turned to Peter. "How will I make the journey the way I am?"

Peter placed his hand over hers. "I'll take you there, child."

Susan sat silent then while the boy read the letter again and again for those who came to hear what it said. America was far away, but Australia was beyond imagining. A land where people walked about upside down, the boy said, without falling off the earth.

Late that night Peter came and called Mama urgently. "Come quickly, she needs you," he whispered. "It's her time."

"Marya, you come too," Mama said. She took the black pot from the fireside and went out. Marya dressed and followed. Peter had heaped up driftwood to make a good blaze on the hearth. A pot of water already simmered on the fire. Marya lifted it off the pothook and sat it in the ashes. She filled Mama's pot with water and hung it in its place.

Mama sat beside Susan's bed, soothing her. "There's nothing to be afraid of," she reassured her. Other women came and shooed Peter out of the house. They gathered round Susan, whispering words of comfort and encouragement to her. The night seemed long. Marya dozed by the fire. When she woke, a pale light shone through the cracks in the door. It was morning.

"Has the baby come yet?" she asked Mama.

"No, not yet. Go and get Packey and Breege up," Mama said. Marya remembered. Today was eviction day.

Eight

A troop of policemen came first and stood in
line at one end of the laneway, waiting for
the bailiff to come. "Can't you leave it for
another day?" old Peter asked. "We'll go
tomorrow, but don't put us out today."

The bailiff and the agent arrived on
horseback. The bailiff's men marched behind
them, armed with picks and crowbars. Peter
tried to speak to them but the policemen kept
him back. "Anybody who resists will be charged
with disturbing the peace," the bailiff warned in
a stern voice.

Marya ran next door. "Mama, the bailiff's
here," she whispered. Mama detached herself
from the group of women who surrounded
Susan and hurried back to her own house. What
remained of their possessions was already packed
into a small bundle. Mama had given away
everything else. Marya looked round the house
with its crumbling clay walls and leaky thatch. It

wasn't much, yet all their memories were here. Their memories of Dada most of all. She bit her lip to check the tears which welled up in her eyes and took Packey by the hand.

Their house was first. The bailiff came and stood importantly at the door. He read aloud from a piece of paper and ordered his men inside. There was nothing left in the house for them to carry outside except the red sods of turf from the fire.

The bailiff turned to Mama. "Where is your husband?" he asked.

"I am a widow."

The bailiff hesitated. He looked anxiously at the landlord's agent who stood at a distance, beside the safety of the police line. "A cart is provided for anyone who wants to go to the workhouse," he said in a loud voice. He turned to his men and gave the order: "Set fire to the thatch."

The men looked from one to another. Nobody moved. "You didn't say we were putting out a widow," a man objected.

"That's not your affair. Now, one of you light that thatch."

"You can light it yourself."

"I said, light the thatch," the bailiff repeated in a nervous, high-pitched voice. Still nobody moved.

The agent came forward. "A pound for whoever will light the thatch." There was a long silence.

Mama stepped forward. "I will light it," she said in a quiet voice. She lifted a sod of lit turf and pushed it into the overhanging thatch. For several minutes smoke eddied from the damp straw. The wind stirred among the eddies till a red glow could be seen in the thatch. It quickly kindled to flames and soon the whole thatch was blazing.

Marya felt her eyes burn with smoke and tears. In spite of the intense heat of the burning thatch, she shivered and her teeth chattered.

Mama turned to the agent. "My pound, Mr Hamilton."

The agent groped in his waistcoat pocket, took out a gold sovereign and gave it to her. She went back to Susan's house. Peter let her in. Then he closed the door and stood defiantly before it. "You can't come in here," he said. "There's a woman in childbirth.

As the bailiff's men moved towards him. a scream sounded from inside. The bailiff looked at the agent and the agent shook his head.

"We'll leave that house till last," the bailiff said and led his men to the next house.

One by one, houses were emptied of people and the thatched roofs set ablaze. People stood in stunned silence, watching their homes burn. A few houses were already empty, their occupants gone away. They were quickly set on fire.

Only two houses remained when a terrible cry sounded from Peter's house. The house was already shrouded in smoke and its thatch starting to burn, set alight by sparks from adjoining thatches. Susan's cry was followed by the wail of an infant.

The bailiff's men carried Susan and her baby out on her pallet of straw and laid her on the ground. Mama's shawl covered her. She seemed to be asleep, her newborn infant in her arms. Mama and the other women gathered round Susan to screen her from the men and from the sharp wind. The bailiff and his men set fire to the thatch and turned to go.

Suddenly, old Siubhan rushed out from a smoking doorway. She ran up to the agent and flung herself on her knees before him. Her white hair hung wildly about her head and shoulders. "Alexander Hamilton," she shouted, stretching out her arm and pointing a bony finger. "My curse upon you and my curse upon all belonging to you! You have sons but, I tell you, not one of them will live to carry your name."

The agent flinched as if from a blow. He turned and walked quickly to his horse. Two policemen pushed old Siubhan away. "You'll rue the day," she called, cackling her crazy laugh. She went on laughing as the bailiff and his men hastily gathered their implements and left, followed by the police. Only the man with the horse and cart remained.

"Take this," Mama said, giving the agent's gold sovereign to Peter. "It will help pay for you to take Susan to Queenstown. Ask the carter to let you ride with her to town. You can get her lodging there till she is strong enough to travel."

The men lifted Susan into the cart. Old Siubhan let herself be led to the cart but refused to get in. She broke free from the women who held her and ran, laughing, among the smoking ruins. Eventually they caught her and half-dragged, half-coaxed her into the cart.

Marya climbed in and knelt beside Susan. "Is it a boy or a girl?" she asked.

Susan opened her eyes. "A boy," she said happily.

"What will you call him?"

"Peter, after my father."

Marya sat on the floor of the cart as they drove towards the town. She stroked the baby's head and held his tiny hand in hers. She tried to think only of Susan and the baby. It was better not to think about anything else, not to remember that in one morning everything that was familiar was destroyed. She shivered incessantly and her teeth chattered.

They came to the poorer outskirts of the town where ramshackle hovels leaned together. Peter got down from the cart there and asked for lodging at a low thatched house. The women helped Susan from the cart and went with her to the door of the house. "Please God, we will see each other again," Susan said as they embraced and said good-bye.

Old Peter kissed Mama on the forehead. "You will hear from us," he promised. He kissed Packey and then Breege. Marya cried when it was her turn to say good-bye. Peter held her tightly. "Never fear, child, we'll meet again," he promised.

Marya watched them till they disappeared inside the lodging house. The cart clattered down the cobbled main street, passing the tall houses of merchants and shopkeepers. It crossed the bridge and turned into a winding narrow street before trundling up a steep hill to the workhouse.

"Here you are," the carter said in a cheerful voice when he halted his horse at the workhouse gate. They were expected. A grim-faced porter appeared from a sentry box and opened the iron gate. They passed along a cobbled path. Marya was aware of high stone walls with small latticed windows.

A heavy door opened with a groan. Inside, an imposing gentleman in a black frock-coat and tall black hat stood gazing before him, oblivious of the people at the door. Near to him, seated at a desk, was a small bespectacled man. An inkwell, a pen and a ledger were laid out on the desk before him.

"Stand in line," the porter ordered. The new arrivals lined up meekly against the wall.

The dignified gentleman finally took notice of them and spoke. "Those who wish to apply for admission to the union workhouse may make their application now. Who is first?"

Mama stepped forward.

"Your name?"

"Máire Mac Giolla Bríde."

The bespectacled man glared. "Speak in English when you address the Master," he said sternly.

"Mary Gilbride," Mama repeated in English. The clerk wrote painstakingly.

"Children?"

"Three. Mary, Brigid and Patrick."

The Master inspected the children and turned to the clerk. "Two females. One idiot, male."

"Their ages?"

"Thirteen, twelve and seven."

"Is your husband alive?"

"No."

"Have you any means?"

"None."

"Very well, you will be provisionally admitted until the board examines your case."

The clerk rang a bell. A door opened and two orderlies, a man and a woman, appeared. "One to females' ward, two to girls' ward, one to male idiots' ward," the clerk instructed without lifting his head from his ledger. The male orderly took Packey by the arm.

"Can't he stay with me?" Mama pleaded. "He'll be no trouble."

"Let him go. He has to go where he belongs."

The female orderly held Mama by the arm while the man dragged Packey away. Packey screamed and struggled as the man opened a door and forced him through. The door closed but they could still hear Packey's cries. "This way," the female orderly said, leading Mama into an adjoining room. "You must bathe and change your clothes."

Shivering, they undressed and washed in the tubs of cold water. The orderly offered them damp rags to wipe themselves dry. Mama seemed unconscious of what she was doing. She sighed and shook her head, murmuring desperately under her breath. Marya buttoned Mama's thick cotton blouse, because she had left it undone, and fastened her grey skirt. Mama did not seem to notice when the orderly handed each of them a white smock for wearing over the uniform. Marya helped her put it on, as if she were the mother and Mama the child. "Heaven protect him," Mama whispered to herself and sighed as if her heart would break.

Nine

They stood in line again and waited. The flagstone floor felt cold under their bare feet. Eventually the orderly led them outside across a yard and into a second building. Here they were separated. Women were to go to the female ward and girls to the schoolroom. Mama held Marya and Breege close. "Be good and do as you are told," she whispered before turning to climb up a steep stone stairway.

Breege tried to follow but the orderly seized her. "You have to go to the schoolroom," she insisted, dragging Breege along. Marya followed, trying hard to swallow the lump that gathered in her throat.

The schoolroom was a long whitewashed room. At one end, a small fire glowed on a hearth. Row upon row of pale girls sat on narrow benches. The teacher pointed to a bench by the wall. Marya and Breege sat down and waited till the lesson ended.

"Your names?" the schoolmistress asked.

"Brigid Gilbride."

"Brigid Gilbride, ma'am," the teacher corrected her. "And you?"

Marya struggled to speak her name but her throat constricted with sobs and no words would come.

"Her name is Mary Gilbride, ma'am," Breege said quickly. "We're sisters."

"Can you read?"

"No."

"Then you will have the opportunity to learn while you are here, and also to write."

Marya understood most of what the schoolmistress was saying. She would learn to read. In the workhouse she would go to school. She had never been to school before. The hedge-school in the next townland had cost a penny a day. Nobody in the lane could afford that. Yet surely she was too old now to start learning.

A bell rang. It was time for dinner. The girls lined up and walked in silence along a stone paved corridor. They lined up again inside the dining-hall. An orderly handed out wooden bowls and iron spoons. A second ladled out small portions of yellow meal porridge. A third poured milk on the porridge and gave each pauper a piece of bread.

The girls went to their tables and waited.

Men and boys came in separate files and, last of all, the women. Marya watched eagerly for Mama but could not see her.

When everybody was served they still waited. At last the Master came. He no longer wore a top hat. His head was bald and shone as if polished. He strode to a rostrum at one end of the dining-hall. A small plump woman came behind him, trotting to keep up. She stood beside the rostrum. The Master opened a prayer book and began to read grace in a loud voice.

"Who is that little woman?" Marya asked the girl nearest to her. The girl put a warning finger on her lips.

The warning was too late. The Master paused in his reading. "You, girl. Come forward."

Marya went all the way up the room to stand in front of the rostrum. The Master glared for a moment, then resumed reading. It was a lengthy grace. Marya felt that all eyes were on her. At last the grace ended. There was a clatter of benches and stools as the paupers sat down. The Master turned his attention to Marya. "Your name, girl?"

"Mary Gilbride."

"Don't you know the rule against speaking in the dining-hall?"

"No, sir."

"No?"

Marya's lips trembled.

"I believe she is one of the new admissions," the plump woman said.

"A bad beginning," the Master said sternly.

"Perhaps she doesn't know the rules yet."

"Then see that she knows them before she enters the dining-hall again."

"Indeed. I'll be instructing the new admissions in the rules this afternoon."

The Master turned to Marya once more. "You may go."

"Yes, sir. Thank you, ma'am." Marya went quickly back to her place and sat down. Her porridge was cold and lumpy but she was hungry and ate eagerly. There was no sound in the dining-hall except the scrape of iron spoons against wooden bowls. She carefully scraped her bowl clean. Why were they not allowed to speak? she wondered. She slipped her piece of bread into her sleeve to eat later.

After dinner it was time for exercise. The girls' exercise yard was a muddy space surrounded by high walls. Marya found Breege and they stood together, watching other girls walking round and round. A small thin girl whose brown hair was plaited in long braids stopped beside them. "You must walk. You'll be punished if they see you standing about."

"Punished?" Marya did not understand.

"Don't you speak English?"

"Not very well."

"Then we'll talk Irish." She changed languages. "You can walk with me if you like. My name's Rachel."

"I'm Marya. This is my sister Breege."

"You'd better start walking." Rachel walked in the middle between Marya and Breege. "Don't go so fast. We'll get tired," she said. The exercise period lasted half an hour, but Breege had so much to ask that the time passed quickly. Marya said little but listened attentively.

"Why can't we talk at meals?"

"The Board of Guardians makes the rules. Lots of rules."

"Who are they?"

"They're the gentlemen in charge. We never see them. They meet in the boardroom and tell the Master and the Matron what to do."

"Is the Master always so stern?"

"Most of the time. Matron is fair but the Master is always looking for excuses to punish people. If he catches you breaking rules, he cuts your food allowance or sends you to the refractory room."

"The what?"

"The refractory room. It's a sort of cupboard where they lock you up."

"Were you ever locked up?"

"No, but my sister was." Rachel pointed to a dark-haired girl who walked all alone, seeming to avoid the company of others. She was taller than Rachel. "Her name's Hannah. She's nearly fourteen, two years older than me."

"What did she do?"

"I don't know. The Master said she was disobedient but she wouldn't tell me anything about it."

Marya asked the question which was uppermost in her mind. "When do we see our mother?"

"You're not allowed to see her."

"Not ever?"

"It's against the rules. What it really means is that you can't talk to her. You'll see her in the dining-hall sometimes. If you're sent to work in the kitchen or the laundry, you might see her there. Even if your mother's not there you can ask someone to give her a message. It's against the rules, but they can't catch you."

"Do you ever see your mother?"

"My parents are dead. There's just me and Hannah."

"You must miss them?"

"Sometimes. In the chapel when mothers and fathers are trying to see their children, there's never anyone looking for me or Hannah."

"Will we see Mama in the chapel?"

"On Sundays. But don't try to talk to her. Don't even make a sign. The porter spies all the time to try to catch people."

"Is he the man at the gate?"

"Yes. Keep away from him. He likes to pinch the girls. They say he beats the boys when he's drunk."

Marya pondered this information. Her new world seemed filled with intimidating grown-ups.

Ten

They went back to the schoolroom. It was time for work. A table heaped with hessian ticking cloth was pulled out from the wall. Each girl took a piece of work and a packing-needle. Marya and Breege were given a mattress cover to sew.

They knew how to sew. There had always been mending and darning at home, but they had never worked with ticking before. There were no thimbles for pushing the needles through the tough material and soon their fingers ached.

"Rub the needle with your hair," Rachel said. "That will make it pass through more easily."

It sounded odd. Marya rubbed the needle in her hair and found that it became oily and passed easily through the cloth. With quick deft stitches she sewed the length of a seam.

The schoolmistress came to inspect the work. "You girls sew very neatly," she said approvingly. "Can you do anything else besides plain sewing?"

"Pin stitch and sprigging," Marya said. In the lane, the women were skilled at needlework and knitting. Sometimes drapery shops in the town gave out fine work to be done. At other times, ladies of the gentry gave orders for needlework. Marya and Breege had helped Mama sprig the borders of bed-linen when the agent's daughter was to be married and a trousseau was made. There were dozens of beautiful pillowcases of fine linen with matching sheets and valances. Marya remembered how astonished she was that anyone should sleep in such finery.

As she sewed, she thought of the evenings when the women gathered together in one house and sat in a circle round a single candle singing and telling stories while they worked. Mama sang her best songs and sometimes Marya or Breege was called on to sing in their turn. Abruptly she remembered that there would be no more such evenings. It was all gone. Gone for ever. She stopped sewing and wiped her eyes.

Just as sewing time ended, an orderly came to tell the girls who were newly admitted to report to Matron. The Matron looked smaller and plumper than she did when she was standing beside the high rostrum in the dining-hall. The girls stood before her as she read the workhouse rules.

"Inmates must wash every day. You must keep your clothing clean. Your hair should be combed every morning and tied back. Combs are provided in the ward for this. Speaking is not allowed at mealtimes nor in the ward after nine o'clock. You may not speak to inmates of other wards at any time. No swearing, smoking or drinking of alcohol is permitted. No fighting will be tolerated. Food may not be removed from the kitchen or dining-hall."

The Matron read quickly in English. Marya had difficulty in understanding all of what she said. However, she understood what she said about not taking food from the dining-hall and thought guiltily of the piece of bread which she had hidden in her sleeve. She put her hands behind her back and felt for it. Suddenly the Matron's eyes were on her.

"Girl, stand straight, hands by your sides."

She put her hands by her sides and heard the bread fall on the floor.

"Step forward, girl." Matron shook her head. "You again!"

"I didn't know it was against the rules."

"Pick it up. I hope you are not going to be a troublesome inmate."

"No, ma'am."

"I'm glad to hear that. Now, eat the bread at once and remember in future that you do not take food from the dining-hall."

Supper consisted of another bowl of gruel.

Only the children were given supper. They lined up for their portions and waited. This time the Master did not appear. The Matron said grace. There was a clatter of iron spoons and, in a few minutes, all was eaten.

Matron read night prayer and dismissed them. An orderly carried a lamp to light their way up the stairs to the girls' ward. The ward was a long room with mattresses laid on long raised platforms. The only empty space was the gangway between the platforms. At one end, beneath a small latticed window, sat an enormous iron chamberpot. Marya and Breege waited to be told where to sleep.

Marya counted the mattresses while she waited. She got muddled after she counted to sixty. She was never very good at counting seventies and eighties. "Here's your bed," a second orderly said. She gave Breege a rolled mattress and Marya a blanket. They pushed mattresses aside to make an empty space on the platform. Quickly they slipped off their skirts and lay down as they saw the other girls doing, one at the top and one at the bottom. They spread the blanket over them.

"No talking," the orderly reminded them. She took the lamp and left the ward. There was the sound of a key turning in the door lock. Marya realised they were locked in. She lay in the darkness feeling loneliness flood over her. In one day her whole world had changed. She was in a strange place, with only Breege for company, sleeping in a room full of strangers. At home there would have been a glow among the ashes in the hearth to light the darkness, but here all was pitch black.

Quietly she twisted herself round and crawled up the bed till she was lying alongside Breege. Breege lay still. Perhaps she was asleep already. Marya curled up close to her till her cheek was against hers. Breege's cheek was wet.

"Are you crying?" she whispered.

"Yes."

"So am I."

They put their arms around each other and cried together till they fell asleep.

Eleven

In the morning they were awakened by the clang of a bell. Marya started up. It was still dark. A gleam of light came through the open door from a lamp hung in the stairwell. Marya groped in near darkness for her skirt and hastily pulled it on, wondering if it was right side out. Then there was squabbling over the steel combs which were hung behind the door and had to be used by everybody in turn. Breege and Marya were last to have a comb. They combed their hair and tied it back as the Matron had directed. Perhaps there would be time later to plait it. They lined up with the other girls at the door and waited to be told to go downstairs. Light streaked the eastern sky as they went outside into the girls' yard.

It had rained heavily in the night. There were filthy puddles around the pump and the latrines where open drains flooded the yard. Breege and Marya waited for their turn at the latrines, standing well away from the puddles and the stench which rose from them. Then they queued at the pump and washed as best they could under a meagre trickle of water.

"There's always a shortage of water," Rachel said. "In summer they carry it in barrels from the river."

Marya let the water flow on her muddy feet while Breege pumped. Then Breege took her turn while Marya pumped. They saw that the other girls rubbed themselves dry with their sleeves and their skirts, so they did the same.

They lined up once more and went to the chapel for roll-call and morning prayer. Both the Master and Matron were present. The girls were inspected. Matron sent some back outside to wash their feet properly. After prayers they went for breakfast, another bowl of yellow meal porridge. The best thing about the workhouse, Marya thought, was that there was something to eat at every mealtime. If they could see Mama and Packey sometimes, it would not be too bad.

After breakfast, Matron allocated the day's work. Breege was sent to help in the laundry. Marya went with Rachel's sister Hannah to scrub the front stairs and lobby. "Hannah will show you what to do," Matron said.

Marya followed Hannah to the washhouse near the laundry. "I'm Marya. I know your sister,

Rachel," she said. Hannah did not reply. She took a bucket from the row of buckets hung along the wall and handed it to Marya. Then she took one for herself and selected two blocks of sandstone for scrubbing. She turned abruptly and went towards the rear of the building.

"Where are we going?" Marya asked.

"To the laundry."

Marya followed and found that they had to get soap and floorcloths in the laundry. They filled the buckets at the pump in the girls' yard and carried the water to the front building. "You start scrubbing here," Hannah said, pointing at the flagged floor of the entrance lobby.

Marya looked in bewilderment at the vast expanse of flagged floor. Where would she begin? Hannah was already climbing the wide wooden stairs.

"I don't know what to do."

Hannah paused and turned. "Haven't you ever scrubbed a stone floor before?"

"No."

"You rub soap on the sandstone and scrub forward and back. Use plenty of water and then wipe. Start at the front step." It was the longest speech she had made so far.

Marya carried the heavy bucket of water to the front doorstep, slopped water with the cloth and began to scrub. She realised quickly that the sandstone block would blister her hands and held it in the cloth as she scrubbed forward, back, forward, back.

She could hear Hannah scrubbing upstairs with the same motion. Forward, back, forward, back. She wondered how many women and girls, all over the workhouse, were scrubbing just now, going forward and back, scrubbing with sandstone on wood and stone. Was Mama somewhere scrubbing?

Her hands grew numb with cold and her arms ached. In time, she supposed, she would get used to scrubbing. At home the floor was made of trampled earth and did not have to be scrubbed. All it needed was a light brushing towards the hearth with a heather twig.

She eased her back and bent to scrub again. Forward, back, forward, back. Upstairs a door opened and she heard the Master's voice. "Hannah, come here." Hannah's sandstone still sounded, forward, back, forward back.

"Hannah," the Master said more loudly.

The scrubbing stopped. Then she heard Hannah. "No, sir, I don't want to. No."

A door slammed. Marya listened but could not hear Hannah scrubbing any longer. She resumed scrubbing the wide flagstones, forward, back, forward, back.

When Hannah came downstairs she was

silent as ever. They carried the buckets of dirty water to the yard and emptied them into the drain. As they put the buckets and cloths away, a grey-haired woman drew close to Marya and spoke in Irish.

"Are you Máire Mac Giolla Bríde?"

"I am."

"Your mother asks are you well."

Marya's heart leapt. "Yes, I am well. Tell Mama we are both well. How is she?"

"She is well but she misses her children." The woman moved quickly away and Marya went with Hannah to the schoolroom. She felt enormous relief. It was as Rachel said. They were not totally cut off from Mama. They could send messages.

In the schoolroom, Rachel was a monitor. Her task was to teach the alphabet to those who did not know how to read. Marya and Breege took their places on a long bench which they shared with some very small girls and several older girls who, like themselves, were unlettered.

"A," Rachel said, pointing at the letter on a chart on the wall.

"A," the girls repeated in unison.

They recited the whole alphabet, all the way to Z. Then they repeated it all over again. They used slates to copy the first three letters over and over. Then they rubbed the slates clean and started again with the next three letters.

Marya worked painstakingly, repeating the sounds to herself. At first it was difficult to make the letters accurately but she improved quickly and, by the end of the lesson, she could write them neatly without looking at the chart.

"You're better than me at it," Breege said ruefully as she wiped out a lopsided "B" and tried again.

The door to the schoolroom opened. A hush fell on the girls. Two elderly ladies entered the room. Their skirts rustled and were almost too wide to let them pass through the door. The Master followed, bowing obsequiously. "Miss Agnes Browne and Miss Laetitia Browne," he announced. Miss Agnes was tall and thin. Miss Laetitia was plump, with soft curves and dimpled cheeks. "You may leave us now," Miss Agnes said to the Master. Still bowing, he withdrew.

"We should like a few moments with the girls," Miss Laetitia said. Miss Keenan nodded. Miss Laetitia passed between the rows of girls, presenting each girl with a lump of sugar. "Pop it in your mouth. It is to sweeten your voices," she said.

Miss Agnes followed Miss Laetitia, giving a printed leaflet to each girl. "Now we shall sing," she announced when everybody had a leaflet. She began to sing in a shrill quavering voice.

Miss Laetitia waved her arms. "Everybody sing," she urged. "Let us praise the Lord." The girls sang, feebly at first but more confidently as they picked up the air. Marya could not read the words on the leaflet but sang without words to please the old ladies.

When they came to the end of the hymn Miss Laetitia nodded with delight. "Lovely, quite lovely."

Miss Agnes looked solemn. "Let us now thank the Lord for his blessings," she said, joining her hands and bowing her head. Miss Laetitia did the same. The girls bowed their heads. After a short silence, Miss Agnes raised her head. "That will do now. Thank you, Miss Keenan. Thank you, girls."

"You've all been very good," Miss Laetitia said. She turned and followed her sister through the door, turning sideways to accommodate her wide hooped skirt.

"Who are they?" Marya asked Rachel.

"The two Miss Brownes. Charitable ladies from the town. They visit quite often."

Towards the end of lesson time Miss Keenan examined Rachel's group. They chanted the letters in unison, Marya calling them out clearly towards the end of the alphabet when the others hesitated. She was pleased to discover that she could learn so quickly.

After dinner it was raining heavily. Instead of exercise they had extra sewing time. Miss Keenan gave Marya and Breege squares of cotton and coloured threads to make samplers of what fancywork they could do.

Marya asked for scissors. She carefully scalloped the edges of the cloth and worked a delicate border on the sampler. Breege hemmed a piece of cloth with small stitches and ornamented the stitches with coloured thread. Then she worked an inner border of cross-stitch three rows deep.

Rachel brought her mattress cover over and sat with Marya and Breege. All around them girls talked quietly. Marya noticed that only a few girls spoke Irish and then very softly, for fear of being reprimanded. The rest spoke English. Marya learned English words quickly. She listened intently, seldom speaking but hearing everything that was said around her.

"What does it mean?" she asked Rachel when a word baffled her.

"You're so stupid," Rachel teased but she then gave in and explained it.

Twelve

During the weeks which followed, Marya and Breege became accustomed to the routine of the Workhouse. They did as they were told. Their day was filled with lessons and work so time passed quickly.

On Sunday Marya glimpsed Mama just once as she walked in line into the chapel. Mama was with the women at the back of the chapel. She saw Marya at the same instant that Marya saw her and their eyes met for a second before Marya was obliged to move on and take her place in the girls' section of the chapel.

For almost an hour a priest intoned in Latin. He gave a short sermon in English, admonishing the paupers to be obedient and humble. Marya noticed that he was plump and well-fed, like the Master. His hands were soft and white. When the service ended several people pressed close to speak to the priest, but he waved them impatiently away and left the chapel.

Rachel did not go to chapel with Marya and

Breege. She went later when the minister of the Established Church came. Protestant children each had a catechism and a Bible. "It must be wonderful to have books of your own," Marya said.

"Not if you have to learn reams of scripture," Rachel said in disgust.

On Sunday no work was allowed. When Rachel came from service and Sunday school she sat reading from her Bible.

"What is your book about?" Marya asked.

"It's mostly stories."

"Stories? What kind of stories?" Marya had heard stories at firesides but she had never heard a story from a book.

"I'll read you one," Rachel said. As she read, several smaller girls gathered around. The story was about a man called Jonah who was swallowed by a whale and lived inside the whale for three days and three nights.

"It's not true, is it?" Breege asked.

"Oh, yes. Everything in the Bible is true."

"He lived inside a whale for three days and three nights?"

"That's what it says."

"When I learn to read I'm going to read that book myself," Breege said suspiciously.

Next morning Marya found herself sitting beside Hannah at breakfast. Marya was halfway through her bowl of porridge when Hannah suddenly stood up and left the table, leaving her breakfast untouched.

A girl reached for Hannah's bowl. Marya seized the bowl and drew it close to her own. "You can't have it. I'm minding it for her," she whispered fiercely.

She really did mean to keep the porridge safe for Hannah till she came back. She waited for a while but then she realised that there would not be time for Hannah to come back to eat it. She pushed away her empty bowl and ate Hannah's porridge.

Marya and Rachel were on laundry duty that morning. They were sent to carry buckets of water from the pump to the laundry. "What's wrong with Hannah?" Marya asked.

"She's sick. Matron sent her to the infirmary."

Marya felt guilty. Perhaps she should have shared the porridge with Rachel. But Rachel was sitting at a different table. It would have been impossible to pass the porridge to her.

Marya liked laundry duty. It meant pumping water in the women's yard and carrying buckets of water into the laundry room. There might be a chance of seeing Mama there, or perhaps someone with a message from her. She would have liked to send a message but was afraid to ask any of the women.

The best part of the day was lessons in the schoolroom. Already she could read and write simple words now and add up figures which she wrote painstakingly on her slate. Breege learned more slowly. Letters and figures irked her. "I don't want to learn," she argued when Marya tried to help her. "What use is it?"

"Some day you might want to write a letter or read one."

"You can write it for me. Or read it."

"You just have to try harder."

"I'll write the letters on your slate and you can copy them," Rachel offered.

"All right," Breege said with a sigh.

The weather was wet and cold. There could not be any exercise in the yard while it rained so the girls stayed in the schoolroom and did sewing all afternoon. As the light faded they sat close to the windows to make use of the last of the daylight. Then, when it was almost dark, thick tallow candles were lit and placed in wall brackets so that they could go on working till suppertime.

In the semi-darkness, an excited whispering began. It spread through the room as a tale was passed from one girl to another. Then it grew to a commotion. Girls gathered in groups to whisper together and look furtively at Rachel.

They passed forward and back on trivial pretexts, to thread a needle close to the candle or to fetch more thread. As they passed, they paused to whisper to Rachel. Marya did not understand the words which were flung with such spite.

"Your sister is a whore."

"Trollop."

"Slut."

Rachel hissed angrily, "No, she's not."

There were more whispers. Rachel flung angry words back. Miss Keenan looked with a frown in her direction. Rachel suddenly flung herself on a small thin girl whose taunts were more vicious than the others. The two girls screamed and tugged each other by the hair. A tall red-haired girl pounced on Rachel from behind. "Fair play," Marya called out in Irish. She seized the girl's red hair and tried to drag her away from Rachel.

Furious, the girl turned and punched Marya on the ear. Marya lashed back but her attacker was bigger and stronger. She forced Marya to the ground.

"Stop this at once," Miss Keenan ordered. "What is the reason for this behaviour?"

Rachel panted with rage. Marya stood up and straightened her smock.

"It was her fault," said the small thin girl, pointing at Rachel.

"I was trying to stop them fighting," said the red-haired girl.

Miss Keenan turned to Rachel. "Well, Rachel? What have you to say for yourself?"

Rachel did not speak.

"What is your excuse, Marya?"

Marya wanted to explain that Rachel had been insulted but she did not know the meanings of the words which had been used and could not be certain that they were insults. She struggled to find the proper words in English but failed.

"If you will not answer, I must suppose that you two are to blame. Go upstairs at once to the ward. You will have no supper."

Rachel went silently towards the door. Marya followed. Upstairs in the ward, Rachel ignored Marya and lay face down on her bed. "Pay no attention to them," Marya said. Rachel did not reply.

Later, in the darkness, after the lamp was taken away, the whispering started again. The story grew and spread and although Marya refused to listen, Breege heard it. "They say that Hannah is with child, that she has been moved to the women's ward," she whispered.

"Don't listen to them," Marya said angrily. "Put your hands over your ears."

"I wonder who is the father?" a voice asked out loud in the darkness.

"Maybe it was the porter," came a reply. Voices gleeful with malice tittered all over the ward.

Marya ached with misery for Rachel's sake. If only she could speak to Mama and tell her what was wrong, she would know what to do.

Thirteen

Marya and Rachel were sent to do yard duty in the morning as punishment for fighting. Their task was to clean the drains and latrines. They were provided with forks and shovels for filling buckets with the filth from the drains. The buckets had to be carried to the cesspit at the back of the Workhouse.

A thick scum floated on the top of the drain. When Marya disturbed it with the fork the stench made her feel faint. She drew back, held her breath and tried again. This time she managed to plunge the fork in deeply and drag out some of the foul-smelling sludge that lay in the bottom. She put it into the bucket and carried it through the laundry, taking care not to let any splash on to the flagstone floor. The back door of the laundry opened on to a walled enclosure which had a huge cesspit at one end. She emptied the bucket there and went back to fill it up again. Rachel worked silently, filling her bucket and carrying it away.

"Your mother asks are you well," a voice said in Irish as Marya passed through the laundry with a second bucketful.

Marya recognised the grey-haired woman who had spoken to her before. She pounded a steaming pot of clothing with a thick wooden beetle. Her face perspired and strands of steel-grey hair lay damply on her shoulders. She spoke without looking towards Marya.

Marya lowered the bucket to the ground and stooped to tuck up her skirt. "Tell Mama we are well. How is she?"

"She is well."

Marya picked up the bucket and went out through the back door. On her return she stopped to tuck her skirt again.

"Do you know Hannah, the girl who was moved to the women's ward yesterday?"

"The one that is with child?" The woman went on pounding.

"Yes. How is she? Her sister is worried about her."

"She is well enough. I will tell her that her sister asked for her."

"Hannah is all right," Marya reported to Rachel.

Rachel paused in her work. "How do you know?"

She told Rachel of the woman who spoke to her in Irish with news of Mama. She could bring news of Hannah too. "She said she would tell Hannah you were asking for her."

Rachel's eyes filled with tears. "We have never been separated before. I wish she had told me. She didn't have to keep it a secret from me."

"Maybe she didn't want to worry you."

"She should have told me."

It took all morning to empty the drains of the sludge which clogged them. Then they had to throw buckets of clean water down the drains to wash them clean. They missed school because it took till dinner time to scrub the latrines with sandstone and soap. Marya's back ached and her hands were raw. She tried not to think about the smell. To think only how pleased Breege would be when she told her there was another message from Mama.

During the weeks which followed, there were more and more admissions. The dining-hall was crowded and portions of gruel and milk grew smaller and smaller. In the schoolroom there was not enough seating. Girls had to sit on the floor. In the girls' ward they slept three and four to a mattress because there was no longer enough bedding to go round. Rachel moved to share Marya and Breege's mattress and blanket. When there was no more room on the mattresses, straw was laid anywhere that there was an empty space to make a bed.

The charitable ladies came again. Miss Laetitia distributed sugar lumps from a paper bag but there were not enough lumps to go round. "I'm so sorry, I had no idea there were so many of you," she said and looked in dismay at her sister.

"We will give tracts to the girls who have had no sugar," Miss Agnes said. Miss Laetitia distributed printed leaflets. Her usual smiles of delight gave way to a frown. She returned to her sister and whispered in her ear. Both old ladies looked closely at the girls and shook their heads. Miss Agnes turned to Miss Keenan. "We cannot help noticing a certain attenuation among the children," she said. "Are they properly fed? What I mean to say is that the children are thin. Deplorably thin. Are they getting enough to eat?"

Miss Keenan hesitated, then replied, "I really can't say. Perhaps it would be best if you put that question to the Master."

"Yes, indeed we will." Miss Agnes looked again at the girls and shook her head. "The attenuation is quite marked. We will take it up with the Master at once." The old ladies withdrew, carefully manoeuvring their wide skirts through the doorway.

Breege became ill. She had painful sores on her

gums and could no longer eat the coarse yellow porridge which was served at every meal. Her joints swelled. Matron sent her to the infirmary.

Within days a dozen girls, including Marya and Rachel, were suffering from the same ailment. "An epidemic of ulcers of the mouth. Doctor Kelly will see you," Matron said and ordered them to the infirmary. Marya was not as sick as Breege but her joints ached. Her gums were tender and bled easily.

Doctor Kelly came to examine them. He was small and stocky and shouted at Matron as if she were an orderly. "Open your mouth for Doctor Kelly," Matron said sharply as Marya waited nervously to be examined. She opened her mouth wide, staring with frightened eyes as the doctor probed her mouth with thick fingers which tasted of tobacco.

"Open wide. It won't hurt," he said. Marya winced when he touched a tender spot. "How long is it since you have eaten potatoes?"

"Not since September."

"Have you ever suffered from mouth ulcers before?"

"No, sir."

The doctor asked all the girls the same questions and wrote their replies in a leather-bound notebook. "It's all a matter of diet," he said to Matron. "They have eaten nothing but

Indian meal for months. They must have wheaten bread and milk twice a day and vegetable soup for dinner."

"The Board of Guardians will object to the cost."

"Do as I tell you. I will deal with the Guardians."

"Yes, Doctor."

Next day Hannah was brought to the infirmary. She was kept in isolation, in a corner of the room. Her skin was yellow and for two days she lay with fever, exhausted, unable to speak. On the third day she became delirious and had to be tied down for fear she would leave her bed. Rachel was allowed to sit with her and moisten her face with a damp cloth.

When the fever passed its crisis she slept deeply for a day and a night. The following morning she woke up and greedily ate a bowl of gruel which Rachel fed to her. Over the days which followed Rachel sat with her constantly.

When Doctor Kelly came again he was dismayed to find a fever case in the infirmary. "Have you not considered the risk of infection?" he asked Matron.

"The Board's instructions were to use a corner of the infirmary to isolate fever patients."

"How often must I tell you that I am the medical officer? The Board cannot overrule my instructions on medical matters. Do I make myself clear?"

"Yes, doctor," the Matron said meekly. "These girls have improved on the soup and bread diet which you prescribed but the Master informs me that the Board has given orders to discontinue it because it costs too much."

"Has he?" Doctor Kelly looked grim. "I will have a word with the Master."

He inspected the patients. Marya had to open her mouth once more and have her gums prodded. "Much better," he noted with satisfaction and wrote in his notebook. "These girls can go back to their ward but they must continue the soup and bread diet."

Rachel sat with Hannah till it was time to go back to the girls' ward. Their heads were close together. Hannah whispered for a long time to her sister.

Fourteen

They found the girls' ward drastically changed. A deep layer of straw was laid in the gangway as extra bedding. There were so many girls that there was barely space to lie down. The small latticed windows could not be opened. The only fresh air came through four small gratings at floor level in the outside walls.

During the night the room became unbearably stuffy. Marya dozed fitfully, wakened from time to time by the sound of girls bickering over floor space. She was aware too of other sounds, a clamour of shouting and howling somewhere outside, somewhere beyond the workhouse walls.

In the morning she was sent to scrub the front lobby and discovered the meaning of the clamour she had heard in the night. The entrance gate was barred and chained against crowds who pushed and jostled, crying out for mercy, begging to be allowed inside.

"Why do they have to stay outside?" she asked the girls who were working with her. They were both new admissions who had come to the ward while she was in the infirmary.

"The house is full. They can't take in any more people so they are waiting outside."

"My family had to wait five days to get in," the second girl said. "We had nothing to eat all that time. Two people dropped dead. The workhouse refused to take their corpses for burial because they died outside."

"What became of them?"

"I don't know."

When they had finished their work Marya gathered up her sandstone and soap and put them back in the store beside the laundry.

"Will you bring me a bucket of water from the pump?" a voice called out in Irish as she passed by the laundry door. She paused. "Here, girl," the voice said.

Marya went into the laundry and saw the woman with steel-grey hair who carried messages from Mama. The woman did not turn her head. She went on pounding a vat of steaming laundry and spoke again. "Quick, take the bucket and go to the pump. Go at once."

Marya lifted a bucket from inside the door and hurried to the pump. She was halfway across the yard when she saw that somebody was at the pump before her, a woman who sang sweetly in a low voice while she waited for her buckets to fill.

"Mama," Marya said softly but loud enough to be heard. Mama did not turn to look at her, but she spoke Marya's name quietly and then sang again. Marya joined in the song while Mama swung the handle of the pump up and down.

"I heard you were sick," Mama said as she stooped to lift the buckets of water.

"Yes, but we are better now."

"Packey is pining. His heart is breaking at being separated from us."

"When can we go away from here, Mama?"

"Soon it will be summer. The bad times will be over and we will go somewhere that we can be together." Marya's heart sang. She did not ask herself where they would live or how. Mama would take care of all that. She had said they would all be together again. That was enough.

Mama picked up a bucket in each hand. Marya placed her bucket under the pump. "Give Breege my love," Mama said as she moved away. Marya sang Mama's song as she filled her bucket and carried it back to the laundry.

"Thanks, child," said the woman with steel-grey hair. "It will come in useful for something."

Marya smiled at her and the woman smiled back before turning to the steaming vat of laundry once more.

"It wasn't Hannah's fault, it was the Master who did it to her," Rachel announced that night. There was a shocked hush in the ward. "You all wanted to know who was the father. Well, Hannah told me. She says it was the Master."

"I don't believe you," a girl said.

"It's true."

"Don't say things like that. You'll get in trouble."

"He made her come into his room," Rachel persisted. "He made her do whatever he said."

Long after they should have been asleep the girls whispered together. Several gathered round the mattress which Rachel shared with Marya and Breege to hear Rachel tell again what had happened to Hannah.

"It can't be true."

"It is true."

"Perhaps she was raving."

"Yes, she was raving. That's how I found out."

Marya remembered the conversation she overheard between Hannah and the Master on the first morning that she scrubbed the lobby. Rachel was telling the truth. "You must go to Matron and tell her everything," she urged.

"Matron wouldn't believe me. Anyway, the Master told Hannah he would have her put out of the workhouse, and me with her, if she told anyone." She suddenly burst into tears. "I'm so afraid she'll die. My mother died having me."

"She'll be all right," Marya comforted her. She thought of how Hannah looked in the infirmary. The fever left her skin yellow and she was wretchedly thin. Her long dark hair was shorn off, making her look thinner still. If only she could tell Mama. She would know what to do.

Fifteen

In the morning Matron appointed Marya to show two newly-admitted girls how to scrub floors and stairs in the front wing. Marya set the girls to work on the ground floor and went herself to scrub the stairs and the Master's landing. She had completed the upper flight of stairs and started work on the landing when a door opened behind her. She turned to wring her cloth over the bucket and saw two shiny boots before her. She raised her head. The Master was looking down at her.

"Well, little girl, what's your name?" His voice was kind. It wasn't possible that he had done what Hannah said he did.

"Marya . . . that is, Mary," she replied.

"Marya," he repeated as if he had not heard the name in English. "You're new here, aren't you?"

"No, sir, I've been here three months."

"Really?" He looked approvingly. "Such lovely golden hair. Very pretty. Did the Matron tell you to clean my rooms?"

"No, sir."

"Well, the other girls can finish the scrubbing this time. You come in here and do the cleaning."

"Yes, sir. I'll go and get brushes and polish."

She went to the store but there were no dusters there. "Ask Matron," a girl said.

The Matron was busy writing long columns in an account-book when Marya found her in her office. "Silly girl," she said, irritated at being interrupted, "do you think I've nothing to do but find dusters for you? Go to the old women's room and get them there."

The old women's room was next to the schoolroom. The old women sat in rows on narrow benches just like the ones in the schoolroom. They were toothless, with wild hair. She saw old Siubhan, her neighbour from the lane, rocking to and fro and talking to herself. Some of the old women were blind. Others, like Siubhan, had lost their wits. Those who were still capable were occupied with shredding cotton rags into dusters and cloths.

"I need dusters for the Master's quarters," Marya said to an old crone.

"He's got himself another one," the old woman cackled.

Another old women chuckled maliciously. "He picks them younger and younger."

"Should be ashamed of himself."

Marya realised that Rachel's story had spread throughout the workhouse. She quickly chose two pieces of cloth and went back to the Master's quarters. Last night she had believed Rachel's story, but now, in the light of day, she realised how impossible it was. She suppressed the niggling recollection of what she had overheard herself.

"Come in, come in," the Master called out when she knocked at his door.

The Master was looking into a mirror, carefully tying his necktie. He turned to her. "Carry on. I must leave you to work by yourself today. The Board of Guardians is meeting this morning." He straightened his necktie and fixed his shirt collar. Then he put on his frock-coat and top hat and went out, slamming the door behind him.

Marya was relieved that he had to go. She listened to his heavy step descending the stairs and then examined the quarters with care. There were three rooms in all, an office, a sitting-room and a bedroom. The bed was soft, with a feather quilt. The bedroom window overlooked the girls' yard. Marya had not realised that the Master could watch them from his room.

She carefully shook the rugs and swept the floors. When she swept under the Master's bed she almost overturned a large china chamberpot but noticed it just in time. She took it all the way downstairs to the girls' yard to empty it in the drain, then rinsed it at the pump and brought it back upstairs.

She stood for several minutes before a long mirror, looking at her own reflection. She was pleased with what she saw. At home there had been a small cracked mirror which strangely distorted the features reflected in it. Now she saw in the Master's mirror that she was not very tall but quite pretty. And the master was right, she did have lovely golden hair.

She turned away from the mirror and set about dusting the heavy oak furniture and the mantelpiece. There was a pair of china dogs on the mantelpiece. She considered breaking one of them. If she broke one, the Master would hardly let her clean his room again. She held a china dog for a moment, trying to summon up courage to dash it to the floor but could not bring herself to do it.

When she went back to the schoolroom she decided not to mention to Breege that she had cleaned the Master's quarters. After all, nothing had happened. However, at exercise time there was whispering and pointing. Marya knew that the old women, or perhaps the girls who worked with her, had spread the story that she had been in the Master's quarters.

Breege heard the whispers. "I can't believe that you would do such a thing," she said in outrage. "Surely you know better than to go in there. You heard what Rachel said about him."

"But nothing happened. He had to go downstairs to a Board of Guardians meeting."

"You must never go there again."

"But what if he orders me?"

"You must refuse. I will tell Mama if you go there again." Marya tried to dismiss the matter from her mind. After all, it might be weeks before she would be sent to scrub in the front wing again.

She was mistaken. In the morning, when the girls lined up to be allocated their chores, Matron left Marya to last. "The Master is very satisfied with the way you cleaned his quarters. He would like to have you do it every day," she said.

Marya looked round in panic. Breege was already gone about her work. "No," she said faintly.

"No?"

"I won't do it. I don't want to."

There was a shocked hush. Girls who were going to fetch buckets and brushes stopped and listened.

"You don't want to?" Matron sounded more astonished than angry. "Did you say that you don't want to?"

"No, ma'am, I don't want to."

Matron stared for a long time. Then she

noticed the girls who stood about listening. and spoke sharply. "You girls, go about your work. All of you." She closed the door after them and turned to Marya once more. "Now, girl, what is the matter. Are you sick?"

"No, ma'am."

"You realise that if you refuse to work you will receive no food ration?"

"I don't mind working. I'll clean the latrines. I'll do anything, only don't ask me to go to the Master's quarters."

"Don't be silly. You've been there already. Did anything frighten you?"

"No, ma'am."

"Then what's the matter?"

"I'm afraid of the Master. I'm afraid . . . " Her voice faltered and she said no more.

"Well?"

"Hannah used to clean his rooms."

"What are you trying to say, girl?"

"Hannah says it was the Master who made her . . . she didn't want to. I heard her saying she didn't want to, but he made her come into his rooms."

The Matron did not speak for a moment. "You realise that this is a grave accusation? Do you know the penalty for circulating lies and rumours?"

Marya was silent. Matron thought for a moment. "Do not speak of this to anyone. Go and help your sister for today."

Sixteen

Marya obeyed Matron and said nothing, but the rumour spread. Other rumours followed. The girls heard from a kitchen orderly that adult male paupers jeered at the Master when he inspected the male wards. Boys threw stones at the Master as he crossed the boys' yard. His tall hat was knocked off his head into the mud.

The Matron sent for Marya. "The Board of Guardians is to investigate allegations made against the Master. I have been instructed to inform you that you will be called as a witness in the matter."

"Me?"

"I have reported your allegations. And I have spoken to Hannah. She will be a witness also." Matron clasped her small hands. "It is a very serious matter. You will have to take an oath."

"I don't understand."

"You must swear to tell the truth."

"About Hannah?"

"About what you overheard."

During the days which followed Marya brooded anxiously. Would she understand the questions which she would be asked? Would the Guardians believe her?

On Saturday the board met as usual. Marya and Hannah waited downstairs until Matron was sent for them. Marya was awed at the splendour of the boardroom. There was a massive table made of dark heavy wood. The gentlemen sat in high-backed chairs and gazed curiously at Hannah. The Master stood near the head of the table. He wore an embroidered waistcoat and a solemn black coat.

Marya was conscious of her bare feet and of Hannah's wretched appearance. Hannah's smock was too tight for her and bulged indecently. The hem of the skirt had ravelled and hung lopsidedly. Her shorn hair had begun to grow but it was still short, like a boy's.

The gentleman at the head of the table read a document full of incomprehensible words and then Matron was asked to state her grounds for reporting allegations made against the Master.

A gentleman interrupted. "Should the Matron not be required to take the oath?"

Matron placed her hand on the Bible and swore to speak the truth. Then she repeated briefly what Marya and Hannah had told her.

"You believe these paupers?" a gentleman asked. He looked with contempt at the two girls.

"It is not my place to judge whether or not they are telling the truth."

"You are aware that these allegations have given rise to insubordination in the house?"

"I have heard rumours."

"Are you prepared to admit that these allegations are malicious and unfounded?"

"It was my duty to report the matter to the Board, since the girl concerned is under my supervision."

"You deny any malicious intention?"

"I believe I have done my duty as Matron."

Hannah was next. The gentlemen questioned her closely. Marya listened attentively but did not understand all of the questions.

"What is your age?"

"Fourteen."

"What is your religion?"

"Established church."

"How long have you been in the house?"

"Three years."

"Are your parents alive?"

"No."

"You claim that you have had illicit relations with the Master. With how many other men have you had illicit relations?"

Hannah looked bewildered.

"Answer the question. How many?"

"I don't understand."

"With how many others have you engaged in immoral relations?"

The meaning of the question dawned on her. Her pale face flushed red. "None, sir."

"None?"

Hannah shook her head and stood with her head bowed while the Board discussed her answers. At last she was dismissed and stood with Matron.

"Mary Gilbride," the clerk called. He held the Bible to Marya and she swore to tell the truth.

"You have alleged that you overheard a conversation between this female pauper and the Master. Is that so?" the tall gentleman asked.

"Yes, sir."

"What exactly did you hear?"

"The Master told Hannah to come into his room and she said she didn't want to."

"That is all?"

"He told her again."

"I see. And on the basis of this flimsy evidence you assumed that the Master of the house was engaged in illicit relations with a female inmate?"

Marya hesitated. She was not sure what the question meant.

"Answer the question, yes or no?"

"I don't understand the question."

"Did you suppose that anything improper was happening in the Master's quarters?"

"No, but . . . "

"No, you have answered no. That is all we need to know." The gentleman sat down triumphantly.

The gentleman at the head of the table spoke sternly. "It is evident that we have here a conspiracy against the Master of the House, an upright, God-fearing man whose sole interest is the welfare of those in his care. I put it to this Board that these allegations are a fabrication of falsehoods, that they have been brought maliciously, apparently at the instigation of the Matron. I propose that the board report the matter to the Poor Law Commissioners with a recommendation that the Matron be dismissed."

Marya heard Matron's sharp intake of breath. The Master nodded with satisfaction as the proposal was quickly seconded and carried. Hannah and Marya were dismissed from the room.

Seventeen

Two weeks later Matron went away and was replaced by a tall thin yellow-faced woman who wore her grey hair in a tight roll at the back of her head. Her cap and gown were severe and she scowled constantly. Her name was Miss Tievan. She interfered in the kitchen so that meals were served hours late. She discontinued the children's diet and gave orders that they were to have gruel at every meal just like everyone else. She allocated sleeping room in the girls' ward to grown women who bullied and snatched mattresses and straw from the girls.

Several of the new admissions lay sick in the ward for days and she did not come to see them or make arrangements for them to go to the infirmary. The weather was warm and at night the stench of the sick was unbearable.

Each morning she created new chores and left important ones undone. All the girls were put to work each day waxing stairs and floors and polishing brass and iron fittings. The big pots in the kitchen were blacked with pot black and the cost of extra cleaning materials was taken out of the weekly allowance for meal. As a result, the gruel was thin and watery. Essential tasks such as laundering clothes and bedding and cleaning drains and latrines were left undone. The entire house was filled with the smell of overflowing drains.

One morning as the girls lined up for breakfast they heard angry shouts and sounds of furniture being overturned in the dining-hall. The male paupers were rioting. Somebody had thrown a dead cat into the pot of watery gruel and breakfast could not be served. The Master sent for the police. The girls were ushered into the schoolroom but they could hear the uproar in the dining-hall as the police batoned the inmates into submission. Nobody ate that day and, when night came, the girls lay awake in the foul-smelling ward, too hungry to sleep.

Marya was with the group of girls who were sent next morning to wax and polish the front wing. She was carefully buffing the varnished bannister when she heard a heavy foot on the stairs. She turned and found herself face to face with the Master.

"Well, well! Our little eavesdropper, isn't it?"

Marya tried to back away but he took her firmly by the wrist.

"My quarters have to be cleaned. You can do it today, my dear."

"No, I won't." She struggled but the Master held her firmly and dragged her to his door. "I won't, I won't," she screamed as he opened the door and flung her inside.

"Make false allegations, would you?" he sneered, holding her by her two arms and shaking her till her teeth chattered. He raised one hand and struck her hard on the side of the head. Marya screamed and he pressed a hand over her mouth to silence her. She sank her teeth into it. With a curse he let go.

"So you won't do as you're told? A few days in the refractory room will change your mind."

He dragged Marya down the stairs and called the porter from his sentry box at the gate. "Take this girl to the refractory room. Tell Matron she is to stay there for three days."

The porter gleefully pinched Marya as he dragged her along. She dug her elbows into him and kicked his shins. "My, you're a wicked one, aren't you," he chortled as he pushed her into a tiny room and slammed the door. Marya screamed and beat on the door till she was too tired to scream any more. Then she sank to the ground and cried.

The room was only the size of a cupboard. It was not long enough for her to lie down. It was not high enough for her to stand upright. The floor was unpaved damp earth. The only light came through a small ventilation grating high in the wall.

The hours passed and darkness fell. Marya grew icy cold. Her head ached. A fire burned in her stomach yet she shivered with cold. Towards morning she saw light as bright as summer sun enter through the ventilation hole and the refractory room grew warm. Faces floated in front of her. Dada smiled. She saw Peter and Susan and Tom who had gone to Australia and wondered why they had come back again.

Time passed. Sometimes quickly, sometimes interminably. Mama's face came once and Marya asked her for water but Mama did not seem to hear. Why would she not bring water? She called for water again and again. At last there was a scraping of bolts. The door of the refractory room was opened. "Call Matron, she has fever," a voice said. Then all was darkness again.

In the days which followed Marya retched and vomited and doubled up in agony with stomach cramps. She alternated between burning with fever and shivering with cold. Sometimes she was delirious and spoke with old friends who seemed near. Once, she was sure, Mama was by her, bathing her face with water and singing softly to make her sleep. Or perhaps she dreamed that. She could not tell any more what was real and what was a dream.

Time stood still. Periods of light and dark alternated. The ward in which she lay became densely packed with screaming, raving patients who cried out for water and called on God to have mercy on their souls.

As Marya recovered she lay exhausted on a bed of filthy straw, overwhelmed by the smell of the sick and their demented ravings. She realised she must be in the fever shed, where the sick were isolated. An orderly came at intervals with water.

"Does the doctor not come here?" Marya asked.

"There was a young doctor appointed but he took the fever too and died," the orderly replied. "There's not much a doctor can do for fever."

"Does my mother know I'm here?"

"Will you have sense, child. We've more to be doing than sending out lists of who's sick and who's dead." She propped Marya against a wall and fed her a bowl of gruel.

During the days which followed Marya grew strong enough to sit up by herself. The floor of the shed was covered with bodies. Many of the sick had fever. Others had dysentery or the bloody flux. The floor was slimy with excrement and blood. Each day more sick and dying were piled into the ward; men, women and children lying in their own filth and the dead left where they died till Shilling Flanagan came for them.

Shilling Flanagan was the man who took the dead away. He was small and stocky, with a ragged beard and small mean eyes. It made Marya's stomach heave to see him rummaging for corpses. Whenever he found one he dragged it out from among the sick and dying, threw it across his shoulders and carried it away. Then he came back to search for another.

"A shilling a corpse he gets," the orderly said enviously. "Sixpence for a child."

At last Marya was declared free of fever and allowed to leave the nightmare of the fever shed. An orderly helped her walk to the schoolroom and laid her down on a bed of dirty straw. The schoolroom had changed utterly. The long benches were gone and the floor was covered with straw. Pale emaciated women lay on the straw. Marya looked round in dismay. Where were the other girls? They could not all have died of fever. And what about Breege? "Where are the girls?" she asked the orderly.

"Doctor Kelly has sent all the children out of the workhouse."

"Where have they gone?"

"To a house down by the river."

Marya sighed with relief. Breege must be all right. She would be with the others. She must be.

If Breege had been in the fever ward, she would have heard. She wondered about Mama and Packey. Had Mama really brought water or did she just dream it? There was nobody who could carry a message to Mama. She asked the woman who came to carry away the slops if she knew Mama but she just stared and shook her head.

"Water." Marya heard the voice of an old woman who occupied the pile of straw next to her own. Her taut yellow skin seemed too tight for her and showed each bone of her face and hands. Her white hair was matted with filth and neglect. "For God's sake, water," she called again. She spoke in Irish. Perhaps nobody else understood her. With a great effort Marya rose and went to the bucket of drinking water just inside the door. Her head swam and she had to steady herself by leaning against the wall but she managed to fill a bowl and carry it back to the old woman.

"God bless you, child," she said and drank greedily.

During the days which followed Marya tended her. She helped her sit up and eat gruel. She tried to smooth her tangled hair. "What's your name?" she asked.

"Marya."

"That's my name too."

"You're a good girl. God will reward you."

"Why is that child here?" the doctor asked

when he visited the schoolroom. "Stand up girl. Can you walk?"

Marya nodded.

"You should be in the children's house." He made a note in his notebook. Marya had only time to splash some water on her face and smooth her hair as best she could before an orderly appeared and told her to go to the entrance hall.

"Good-bye," she said to old Marya. "Take care of yourself."

The old woman caught her hand and held it for a moment. "Will I tell your fortune?"

Marya hesitated. Did she really want to know her future?

Old Marya did not wait for her to reply. She opened Marya's hand and peered into her palm. "I see sorrow and joy. There is sorrow before you now but, in the end, joy will overcome the sorrow. It is the wind from the east that blows on you now. That is a hungry wind and it has done its worst with you. Soon the wind from the north will blow and that will be a bitter wind. When the wind blows from the west it will carry you across water. Last of all will be the wind from the south which will bring you happiness and friends you never thought to see again." She paused and looked in Marya's face. "It is a good hand and a good fortune before you. Go now, child, and God bless you."

Eighteen

Marya was one of half a dozen children who were led down the steep hill to the children's house. She found it difficult to keep up. Her legs seemed to be ready to give way under her.

"Here, let me help you," said a red-haired boy. He spoke in Irish. Marya stared for an instant and recognised him. He was Seamus, the boy from the next townland, the boy who knew how to read in English and French and Latin and Greek.

"Don't you remember me?" she asked.

"Should I?"

"You read a letter for us in the lane."

He stared. Then he smiled in recognition. "You've changed."

"I had fever."

"Yes, you look as if you did. You've hardly enough skin to cover your bones." He screwed up his face into a comical grin.

Marya laughed. "Were you sick?"

"I had the squirts."

"What?"

"Dysentery."

He took Marya's arm and let her lean her weight on him. They walked side by side, following behind the smaller children. The orderly led them to a tall house with steps leading to the front door. He lifted the brass knocker and struck the door. A girl opened it. Seamus helped Marya up the steps and turned to follow the orderly to an adjoining house.

"Till we meet again."

"Thanks."

The girl who opened the door led Marya and the other newcomers upstairs to a large room spread with mattresses. "There's your bed," she said, pointing out a mattress to Marya. It was directly below a tall wide window which was open, letting clean fresh air into the room.

Marya stood on the mattress and looked out. The window overlooked the waterfall and the harbour pool below. Far away, she could see the river bar and beyond that the sea. She breathed deeply. The smell of the sea was on the breeze. She could shut her eyes and imagine that she was back in the lane, smelling the salt wind blowing from the sea.

"Marya!" She heard voices and running feet.

The door burst open. Breege and Rachel flung themselves into the room. Breege threw her arms round Marya. "Oh, Marya, Marya," she said over and over. "I was so afraid you would die."

Rachel looked her up and down. "You're so thin."

"And dirty," Breege added. "You'll have to have a bath."

Marya noticed that both Breege and Rachel had lost the gaunt look which they had in the workhouse. They were pale but did not look hungry.

"How is Hannah?"

"Her baby died. She wasn't able to come with us here. They made her stay in the women's ward." Rachel's lips quivered.

"She'll be all right," Marya assured her. "She's had the fever already."

"Marya," Breege began and paused.

Marya knew what she wanted to ask. What about Mama and Packey? Were they safe? She did not know. But surely, if anything was wrong, someone in the workhouse would have told her. "I don't know how they are. Nobody could tell me," she said.

They sat on a mattress while Rachel and Breege told Marya how different life was in the children's house. Miss Keenan, the schoolmistress, was in charge. The doctor had insisted on changes in diet and wrote to the Poor Law Commissioners to ask them to force the Guardians to provide proper food.

Each week he called and talked to Miss Keenan about the children's health. He ordered medicines and fresh air. They were allowed to play freely in the garden instead of walking endlessly round and round as they used to do in the exercise yard. There was only a low garden wall separating them from the boys who were in the house next door. Sisters and brothers were allowed to talk to each other.

An orderly came and ordered Marya to an adjoining room where a hot bath and clean clothes awaited her. She was allowed to rest for the remainder of the day and did not go downstairs till suppertime.

Next day, in the schoolroom, she found that she had not forgotten the things that she had learned. She could still write letters neatly on a slate and remember the spelling of simple words. Miss Keenan put her into a higher group with Breege even though she had missed so much while she was sick. She was glad to be learning again.

At writing time Miss Keenan showed how to write a letter. "With a letter you can keep in touch with friends or relatives anywhere in the world," she explained.

Marya raised her hand. "Even as far away as Australia?"

"Yes. It would take a long time for a letter to go to Australia, much longer than to America. Australia is on the other side of the world."

Marya wondered about that. Was Tom really walking about upside down? Did he have to learn to do it when he got there? She wouldn't have believed that there was any such place except that Tom and Susan and Peter had gone there.

Just before noon a hush fell on the schoolroom. A group which was reciting lessons dropped their voices to a murmur and then stopped altogether. From outside came the rumble of wheels on cobblestone.

"The dead-cart," someone whispered. They sat in silence. Some children closed their eyes and covered their ears. Marya turned to look.

"Don't, it's horrible," Breege whispered.

"I'm not afraid." Marya watched as Shilling Flanagan wheeled the dead-cart down the hill. He turned into the street and passed by the window. Corpses of young and old were heaped together. A young girl with long brown hair was slung, half-naked, on top of the pile.

A woman in the street turned away and held a corner of her shawl to her face to avoid breathing the stench of the dead.

Nineteen

In the weeks which followed Marya found her strength returning. She had eaten nothing since her illness except the thin workhouse gruel. Here there was vegetable soup and white bread for dinner. There was creamy rice pudding with milk for supper. The house was crowded with girls but the big windows made the rooms seem light and airy.

Marya's only chore was to supervise smaller girls at play in the garden behind the house. There was a bench under the kitchen window where the noonday sun shone. Marya carried out a stool and sat there practising words and sentences on a slate. Doctor Kelly had looked at her tongue and felt her thin arms. He warned Miss Keenan that she must be allowed to rest.

Sitting in the sun made her almost too lazy to write. It was summer. Soon Mama would take them to a new home. She shut her eyes and pictured their old home in her mind as if it was still there, as if she could go back and find that nothing had changed. She imagined herself walking by the river, coming with Breege from the shore. Now they were turning into the lane. There was Packey running to meet them. And Dada coming home, bringing fresh mackerel for dinner. And Mama, at the door, wondering what was keeping them all.

A voice interrupted her thoughts. "Will you just look at the lady of leisure!"

Marya opened her eyes but saw no one.

"Up here."

She looked up and saw Seamus's red head at an upstairs window of the house next door. "You don't look like someone who's working so hard either," she retorted.

He screwed up his face into his comical grin and waved a dirty cloth in her direction. "I'm cleaning the windows." He heaved himself out through the open window until he was seated on the windowsill, then held the window frame and leaned back precariously to improve his view of her.

"What are you writing?"

"Words."

"What kind of words?"

"Cat, mat, sat."

"I'll test your reading. Write down this word: c-a-i-l-i-n."

Marya carefully wrote the letters.

"Next word, d-e-a-s. Now read out what you've written."

She hesitated and stammered over the unfamiliar spellings. Then she suddenly recognised what they said and felt her face go warm. *Cailin deas.* Pretty girl. She tried to think of a suitable retort but failed.

"Do you want to learn some Latin?" Seamus offered.

"Like what?"

"*Amo,* I love. *Amas,* thou lovest."

Marya blushed for a second time. She was furious with herself for being so tongue-tied. The tinkle of a bell sounded from inside. She was glad; it gave her an excuse to end the conversation. It was time to bring the children indoors. "I have to go now," she said.

"Till next time," Seamus called.

At morning prayers, Miss Keenan asked them to pray for the Master. He was ill with fever. Marya shut her eyes and tried hard to pray. Rachel, at her side, nudged her and grinned vindictively. Marya tried not to share in her delight. It would be wrong to wish the Master dead, but what a blessing it would be if he did die. She pushed the thought from her head and tried to pray sincerely but the words were mechanical. Her heart was not in them.

"I hope he dies," Rachel whispered fiercely. "Please God, let him die."

"No, don't say that," Breege said apprehensively. "Bad prayers come back on you."

Miss Keenan overheard. "God doesn't listen to bad prayers," she said. "You must try to be more charitable, Rachel."

Rachel lowered her eyes meekly. However, as soon as Miss Keenan left the room she joined her hands, rolled her eyes heavenward and prayed earnestly once more, "God make the Master die in agony. Send him to Hell for all eternity."

It was a terrible prayer. Marya felt a little frightened at Rachel's ferocity. A curse might not always afflict the person it was meant for. Mama and Packey were still in the workhouse. An evil wish could hurt them instead of the Master.

When she supervised the children outdoors, she went to the end of the garden to look at the river and the harbour pool beyond. The harbour had been bustling with activity for days. A crowd of emigrants waited on the quayside, while a timber boat from Canada unloaded its cargo and completed its preparations for taking them on board. Their luggage, barrels of dry food, trunks and bundles were piled on the quay.

The boat was shabby, its sails ragged and

stained with weather and age. Marya remembered when timber boats carried ballast back to Canada. Heaps of smooth round ballast stones still lay on the quaysides. Now there was no need for ballast. There were so many people who wanted to emigrate that passengers were used instead of ballast.

The ship was almost ready now. In a day or two, it would be piloted down river on the morning tide. It would cross the bar, sail past the strand, the rocks and the cluster of tumbled houses in the lane. Then it would cross the ocean.

"Did you hear the news?" said a voice.

Marya started. It was Seamus. He had approached silently on the boy's side of the wall.

"What news?"

"They say the Master's recovering from the fever."

Marya felt deep disappointment. It was wrong, she knew, but she could not make herself feel glad.

"Damn his soul," Seamus added.

"Don't say that."

"Why not?"

"It's not lucky."

They were silent for a moment. "I'm leaving tonight," Seamus said.

Marya turned in astonishment. "Leaving?"

"I've been watching that ship. Those people on the quays are emigrating. They'll be able to start a new life in America. They might be going to New York. A lot of people from my townland went to New York."

"They're not going to New York. That ship is from Canada."

"How do you know that?"

"My father was a fisherman. He knew all the boats coming and going. That's a timber ship from Canada. They're fitting it out for passengers now."

"What difference does it make? New York, Canada, it's all America. Any place would be better than here."

"You'd need money to buy a ticket."

"There should be plenty of places to hide on a big ship like that."

"You wouldn't dare!"

"I would, too."

"It's against the law to stow away. They would put you in jail."

"I could hide till they're at sea. They'd hardly send me back."

"You're daft."

"I'm not going back to the workhouse, that's for sure."

"What about your family?"

"They're dead."

"You'd be caught."

"No, I wouldn't."

Marya looked at his freckled face and frowned. Surely he wasn't serious.

"If I don't get on that ship, I might get on one going to England."

"You're really thinking of going?"

"Yes, I am."

Marya was silent. Could he not see that his scheme was madness? He would need food and money. He talked as if Canada was in the next townland.

"Will you come out here tonight to say good-bye to me?" he asked. "It would be lonely to go away with no one to say good-bye."

"It's too dangerous. How will you get on to the ship?"

"If there's a way, I'll find it. Meet me here at twelve. I'll be waiting for you."

Marya hesitated a moment. "All right," she said.

Seamus smiled, screwing up his nose and his eyes. "See you later."

Twenty

Marya wished she had something to give to Seamus, something useful, to help him on his way. If only she had thought of keeping her portion of bread at dinner. But then, how could she have known at dinner-time that Seamus would need it? Anyway, a single portion of bread would be of little use to him.

The sound of hooves and wheels clattering in the entry at the side of the house caught her attention. It was the baker's van. He came at the same time every day. An orderly came out of the kitchen and unbolted the garden door. The baker's man passed through, carrying a large basket filled with loaves of white bread. The orderly went before him into the kitchen.

Marya had an idea. The enormity of it made her heart thump. The orderly and the baker's man would be in the kitchen till Miss Keenan came down and counted the loaves. She went quickly to the garden door and looked out. The bakers' vans were escorted by policemen now because bakers' vans had been overturned in the main street and robbed by hungry people.

The two policemen were standing in the street keeping a lookout. Their backs were turned to her. Marya opened the door on the side of the van. Inside were shelves stacked with bread. She took out a loaf and hid it under her smock. As she closed the door, the horse stirred. Marya froze. For a few seconds she was sure that she must be caught, but the policemen did not look round.

She slipped back into the garden. The loaf made a peculiar bulge under her smock, but it was not likely that anybody would notice in the time it would take her to find a hiding-place. She went straight to the privy. She pulled straw out of the thatched roof of the little house and made a hole big enough to hide the loaf. Then she covered the bread, carefully threading the straw together so that the hiding-place would not show. Rats would hardly find it before nightfall.

The bell rang. It was time to bring the children indoors. Monitors would give them afternoon lessons while the older girls were sewing in the day room. Miss Keenan would take time to check Marya's lessons and set her more to learn.

As she crossed the hallway to the day room she was overwhelmed by guilt. What if she were found out? The Guardians might blame Miss Keenan. What if she were dismissed for not taking proper care that nobody could steal a loaf? There was no way now to undo what was done. She turned the doorknob and went into the schoolroom.

The girls were sitting cross-legged on the wooden floor stitching industriously. A few who were more skilled at needlework sat round Breege practising the fine embroidery stitches which she showed them. A girl who knew how to crochet lace worked the edge of a handkerchief. The Board of Guardians had refused to supply crochet materials and coloured threads but Miss Agnes and Miss Laetitia had joined with other charitable ladies in the town to provide them.

Marya recited her lesson and Miss Keenan set her some reading to learn from a tattered primer. The passage was easy. Marya could already read the book from cover to cover so she concentrated on learning the more difficult spellings instead of just reading. Her mind wandered a good deal. She thought of Seamus and how glad he would be to have a loaf of bread to sustain him on his adventure. She ignored the feelings of guilt which arose of their own accord in spite of her best effort to suppress them.

That night she forced herself to stay awake. Time and time again she almost fell asleep. In the end, she sat up and waited. Everybody else was asleep. Breege, beside her, was breathing evenly.

At last the town clock struck twelve. She rose and stole to the door. The knob turned with a faint click. It was lucky that they were not locked in here at night, as they had been in the workhouse ward. She went out on to the landing, leaving the door slightly ajar. On the stairs a board creaked. She stood still, her heart thumping. Nobody stirred. Stealthily she went down the rest of the way.

The back door was bolted. The bolt screeched as she drew it back. She stood still again, listening intently for any sound from upstairs. The house remained silent. Carefully she lifted the latch and slipped outside.

It was almost midsummer. The sky glimmered with blue and a faint red glow lit the western sky. She went quickly to the privy. The loaf was where she had left it. Rats had not found it, so far as she could see. She went outside again and down to the bottom of the garden.

Seamus was there before her. She could see him clearly in the semi-darkness. "I brought you a loaf of bread," she whispered and passed the loaf over the wall.

He sniffed it. "Nice and fresh. Thanks. Did you take it from the kitchen?"

"No, I stole it from the bread van."

Seamus reached across the wall and took her hand. He drew her close and kissed her on the lips. "Good-bye," he whispered.

"Good-bye."

He climbed over the boundary wall on to the riverbank, turning one last time to wave good-bye. Marya watched till he disappeared into the night. She went back indoors and crept upstairs. How would Seamus get on board, she wondered. Could he swim? If he could, how would he keep the bread dry?

For a long time she lay awake worrying. She did not think she would be able to sleep but suddenly it was morning. Sunlight streamed in at the tall wide window. Breege was shaking her. "Wake up, Marya, it's almost seven."

She rolled off the mattress on to the hard floor. She remembered Seamus and looked out through the window. The ship was still in the harbour.

That afternoon, she sat in the garden and watched the emigrants line up for medical inspection before being taken on board. She wondered if Seamus had already concealed himself on the ship, or was he waiting for nightfall before making his attempt to board? When the boys came out for exercise they told her the news that Seamus had run away.

At bedtime Marya looked again from her window. The ship was still in the harbour, waiting for the flood tide. The crew would search it thoroughly for stowaways before it crossed the bar. Did Seamus know that? She had not thought to warn him of the search for stowaways.

The following day she heard the rest of Seamus's story. The police had come to the boys' house to inform the schoolmaster. Seamus never reached the harbour. A policeman saw him loitering in a laneway and recognised the workhouse uniform. Seamus was in jail, waiting to be brought before a magistrate. He would be charged with stealing workhouse clothing and having a stolen loaf of bread in his possession.

All evening Marya waited in dread for a policeman to come and arrest her. She wondered should she confess to her part in the crime at once, or would that only make matters worse? If the police did come to arrest her, she would tell the truth, she decided. But if they did not come she would know that Seamus did not want her to be involved.

A knock at the front door made her start. She waited in an agony of suspense while someone went to open it. Nothing happened. Nobody called out her name. A couple of minutes later she heard the front door close.

All evening she listened for the sound of a policeman's knock. It did not come. When it was time for bed she knew that she was not going to be arrested. She could sleep soundly. Seamus had not told.

Twenty-One

A week later the children were moved back to the workhouse. The doctor had delayed their return for as long as the fever raged. Now the Board of Guardians were adamant. There was room in the workhouse for the children. Besides, they had dismissed the new Matron for incompetence and Miss Keenan was needed to act as Matron until someone was appointed.

Marya was glad to be going back. She would see Mama again. It would be enough to see her and know that she was safe and well. She would let them know how Packey was.

They walked two by two up the hill. A light drizzle made everything grey. As they drew near the workhouse, they smelled the stench of the drains. This time there were no clamouring crowds. Only the porter was at the gate, a new porter. Marya wondered at seeing him. Perhaps the old porter was dead. She remembered how he had beaten and pinched her and flung her

into the refractory room. It served him right if
he was dead.

Silence lay over the workhouse. Two by two
they filed through the entrance building and
crossed between the high walls which separated
the children's yards. They fell silent, swallowed
up in the stillness.

The clang of the dinner bell shattered the
silence. They fell back into the workhouse
routine, forming separate lines, one for boys,
one for girls.

"Oh, God," Breege whispered in horror as
they entered the dining-hall. Long lines of
emaciated men and women shuffled forward for
their portion of gruel. The children looked
anxiously, searching for familiar faces.

"Stay in line," an orderly shouted as they
surged forward. They took no heed. Desperately
they searched through the lines of men and
women.

"Mama, Mama," Marya called frantically
because she could see Mama nowhere.

"Rachel!"

"Hannah!"

The two sisters flung themselves into each
other's arms.

Marya went from one woman to another,
looking into each face. The women were
changed. They were thin, with protruding

cheekbones and sunken eyes. "Mama," she
whispered, terrified of the pity in their eyes. A
woman with steel-grey hair took her by the
hand. Marya tried to pull away. The woman
spoke and Marya recognised her voice. She was
the woman who had carried messages from
Mama. "Your mother's not here any more," she
said.

"Is she sick? Where is she?"

"The fever took her. She asked me to tell you
that she will watch over you always."

"Packey? What about Packey?" Breege asked
wildly.

"He died too."

Marya and Breege sobbed loudly, adding to
the confusion around them. Children who
found relatives clung to them, refusing to be
separated. Those who found no one went on
searching, calling desperately.

In the middle of the confusion another sound
arose, a plaintive moan which rose and fell like
waves on the sea. The women were raising a
lament for the dead. The rise and fall of the keen
calmed the children. Their wailing subsided and
they let orderlies lead them from the dining-hall.

"Take the children to their wards," said Miss
Keenan, "they can be fed later." The children let
themselves be led quietly upstairs.

Marya and Breege lay together on scattered

straw. The north wind rattled the latticed windows and whistled high in the chimney. It blew through the ventilation grates and made draughts in corners. Although it was summer they shivered under the thin blanket, not daring to think any more about what the future might hold.

Next day, there was work to be done. The schoolroom was filthy and had to be scrubbed from end to end. The walls had to be painted with lime to prevent infection. A feeble, withered old man with yellow skin and loose clothing came to see what they were doing. It was a moment before they recognised the Master.

"What is this?" he exclaimed. "The Board of Guardians has not authorised whitewashing the schoolroom."

"It must be done," Miss Keenan replied. "This room is full of disease. It must have a lime wash to purify it. The children cannot be exposed to infection."

"But the cost: how can I justify the cost?"

"I believe that the lime we are using costs two pence ha'penny a stone. Much less than medical attendance will cost if the children become sick."

The Master did not seem to have the strength any more to give orders or enforce his objections. He shook his head. "What am I to tell the Board? What will I tell them?"

"Tell them that the medical officer ordered it."

The work provided a distraction from grief. Only one small girl continued to search for her people. She loitered at the door of the schoolroom, going out to look each time a foot was heard on the stairs. She peered through the window when she heard the pump being used in the women's yard.

At dinner-time she did not eat but searched again among the women for a familiar face and then among the men. The men spoke gently to her in spite of the rule against speaking. "Your father and mother are gone," said an old man who seemed to know the child, "but your neighbours are still here. We will take you with us when we go back home."

When Miss Keenan came into the dining-hall the inmates fell silent. She read a short grace. Then she took the small girl by the hand and led her away.

Marya and Breege found that the routine of work helped them get through each day. Night was the worst time. Then they sobbed together till they fell asleep.

Hannah was moved back to the girl's ward and Rachel glowed with happiness to be all day with her sister again. "I was working with your mother in the fever ward," Hannah said. "She asked to be let work there because your brother was sick. Then she got the fever too."

"Did she suffer much?"

"No, she died in a few days. I think she lost heart when your brother died. And she didn't know whether you two were alive or dead. She kept hoping you were alive."

If only they could have let her know, Marya thought. She had promised they would be together. Now they never could be. The thought that Mama had died, alone in the fever shed with no one she knew to nurse her, filled her with misery. Somehow she would have to make a future for herself and Breege. Mama would have wanted that. Somehow, she would find a way.

A new schoolmistress was appointed to take Miss Keenan's place in the schoolroom. She was thin-faced, with a sharp red nose and wore her hair in a tight roll on top of her head. Her name was Miss Gillen.

Instead of writing, the girls learned to recite by heart a long list of prepositions. They also memorised the names of rivers and mountains, imports and exports, oceans and continents. Once Marya raised her hand to ask a question: "Is it true that people walk upside down in Australia?"

"Of course not. Stupid girl." Miss Gillen

interrupted the lesson to draw a circle on the blackboard. She talked about the law of gravity and how it was night in Australia when it was day in Ireland. Marya was bewildered. Was there a law in Australia which obliged people to walk upside down in the dark? She thought about Tom and Susan. They did not know that Mama and Packey were dead. She raised her hand again.

"Could I write a letter to Australia?"

"To Australia?"

"My uncle is there."

"To write a letter you would need writing-paper and an envelope. You would also need the permission of the Board of Guardians."

The door opened. There was a rustle of skirts and petticoats as Miss Agnes and Miss Laetitia came into the schoolroom. Miss Gillen was thrown in a fluster. She curtseyed deeply, hurried to close the door behind them and then lifted a duster to wipe the blackboard.

"No, no, please don't let us interrupt the lesson," Miss Agnes said. "We've heard about your method and have come to see for ourselves."

"Do carry on," Miss Laetitia said with a wave of her hand.

The two charitable ladies seated themselves at the end of a bench and waited expectantly. Miss

Gillen resumed her account of gravity and Australia.

She pointed to the lower end of the circle on the blackboard. "Down here is Australia. It isn't really upside down, although it looks that way. The earth is governed by the law of gravity. Because of the rotation of the earth on its axis, it is night-time in Australia when it is daytime here. Also, due to the rotation of the earth round the sun, it is summer in Australia when it is winter here."

Marya raised her hand. "Ma'am, does that mean that my uncle in Australia is sleeping now?"

Miss Gillen frowned. "Most likely."

Miss Laetitia looked with interest at Marya. "You have an uncle in Australia?"

"Yes, ma'am." On impulse she went on, "I would like to write a letter to him."

"A letter?"

"I have just explained to her, ma'am," Miss Gillen interposed, throwing an indignant look towards Marya, "that she will need writing-paper and an envelope as well as the permission of the Board of Guardians."

"And postage," Miss Agnes added. She turned to Marya. "Do you have the cost of postage, girl?"

"No, ma'am."

"Just as I thought."

Miss Laetitia whispered in her sister's ear. Miss Agnes nodded and spoke to Marya again. "If you wish, my sister Laetitia will write to your uncle on your behalf. What is his address?"

"Australia."

"That's not an address. Did your uncle send any letters home?"

"No, he can't write."

"Do you know anybody else in Australia?"

"His wife, Susan, and her father. I think she went to Australia too. She got a letter saying convicts' wives could go."

"Your uncle is a convict? Then it will be easy to find his address. I will write to the Lord Lieutenant's office and ask." Miss Agnes took a small notebook and a pencil from a little bag which hung at her waist. She wrote down Tom's full name and as much as Marya could tell her about his conviction.

While Miss Agnes wrote, Miss Laetitia went round the room distributing gooseberries from a paper bag. "These are to sweeten your voices," she said brightly. She held out the bag to Marya. The gooseberry tasted sour but Marya tried to look appreciative.

Miss Agnes finished writing in her notebook. She stood up and started to sing in a shrill quavering voice. She seemed to have forgotten that she wanted to see Miss Gillen's teaching method. The girls joined in the hymn and Marya sang as sweetly as she could. "Wonderful, wonderful," Miss Laetitia said, her face beaming with pleasure.

When the door closed behind the two old ladies, Miss Gillen turned angrily to Marya. "How dare you presume to speak to your betters. How dare you!"

"But, ma'am, the lady spoke to me first."

"That is no excuse. You may not speak to visitors without permission."

Twenty-Two

Summer ended and autumn drew in. The potato crop was destroyed by blight for the second time. In the space of a few weeks, the workhouse filled up again. In the girls' ward Marya heard the newcomers sobbing in the night. Sometimes she tried to comfort them. "It won't be for ever," she said to them. "You'll be able to go home some day and be with your family again." As she talked to them, she felt all over again the pain of being separated from Mama and Packey. She remembered Packey's screams as he was dragged away and how Mama grieved. "You will see your family again," she promised the new girls, even though she knew they might not.

In October, a party of gentlemen dressed in black frock-coats and tall hats visited the schoolroom. Marya recognised some of them as members of the Board of Guardians. There was a tall bearded man among them whose face was new to her.

The Master followed the Guardians, bowing

and nodding. Behind him was Miss Keenan. The clerk was last to enter. He carried a pen and paper.

"All those who are aged between twelve and sixteen years and are orphans, stand up," the Master said. There was a commotion. A number of girls stood up.

"Stand in line by the wall." They stood by the wall while the Master counted them. He turned to the bearded gentleman. "Twenty-three in all." The clerk sat down at Miss Gillen's table, drew a pen from his pocket and dipped it into the inkwell.

"As you see, the recent epidemic has left many orphans," the Chairman of the Board said to the bearded gentleman. He turned and pointed at Breege. "You, girl, what's your name?"

"Brigid."

"Brigid what?"

"Brigid . . . your honour?"

"No, no, I mean your surname. What is your surname?"

"Gilbride."

While the Chairman interrogated Breege, the other Guardians walked up and down inspecting the girls. Marya lowered her eyes, embarrassed by their intense scrutiny.

"Are you in good health?"

"Yes, your honour."

"And of good character?" He turned to Miss Keenan.

"I know of nothing against her," Miss Keenan replied, "nor against any of these girls."

Little did she know, Marya thought, remembering the loaf which she stole. Each girl was asked the same questions. Their replies and Miss Keenan's testimony to their good character were noted by the clerk. He wrote furiously, stopping at intervals to dab his words with blotting-paper.

When the chairman questioned Hannah, the Guardians did not seem to recognise her as the same girl whom they had accused of deceit only six months before. Her hair had grown since then, but her name was the same. Could they have forgotten? Marya wondered. The Master looked through the window, his back to the room, while Hannah was answering questions. Did he not want to recognise her?

When Miss Keenan was asked for a character reference for Hannah she answered truthfully, "Since the girl has been in my charge I have nothing to complain of concerning her."

The Chairman of the Board finished asking questions. "I will now give you over to Lieutenant Henry," he said.

The bearded man came forward and spoke. "I have been appointed by the Emigration Commission to select suitable female orphans for emigration to Australia." Marya listened attentively and tried to understand what he was saying. "Each of you will undergo a medical examination. You will require a reference from your minister of religion. Passage to Australia will be free and the Board of Guardians will provide you with such clothing as you will need for the voyage and subsequently in Australia."

Hannah clutched Marya's hand. Marya understood now why the Board of Guardians chose not to remember Hannah. For the price of outfitting her, they could be rid of her from the workhouse. One mouth less to feed. Twenty-three less, if all the girls went. The Guardians represented the ratepayers, not the poor. They would be glad to be rid of them.

"Those of you who are interested in emigrating to Australia stand forward," the Chairman said. Breege looked at Marya and Marya nodded. All twenty-three girls stepped forward.

"Very good. Arrangements will be made for medical examination. Meanwhile, you may obtain references and commence making the clothes which you will need. The Board will provide money for this. I hope that you will be grateful to the ratepayers of this Union who are providing such a splendid opportunity for you."

Marya only half listened. She thought of Tom and Susan. Their baby would be almost a year old now. And Peter, was he with them in Australia?

During the weeks which followed, her feelings

swung between excitement and loneliness. To go to Australia meant to leave home for ever. But where was home? Not the workhouse. Their real home, in the lane, wasn't there any more.

They were excused from housework because there was so much sewing to be done. Six shifts for each girl, two petticoats, six pairs of stockings, two pairs of shoes, two gowns, one of linen and one of worsted wool. There were left-over pieces of cotton which they hemmed and made into handkerchiefs.

"This is a trousseau we're making," Breege said happily. Marya paused in her sewing to think of the time the women of the lane made a trousseau for the agent's daughter. She hummed one of Mama's songs and Breege hummed along with her.

Two dozen straw bonnets were ordered from the draper's in the town and the shoemaker measured each girl for shoes. The excitement of having so many possessions overcame the fear of venturing into an unknown land. Marya tried to convince herself that she really wanted to leave Ireland for ever. Yet she found that, right in the middle of fitting a bonnet or learning to use a button-hook to button her new boots, there were instants when the lane, the seashore and the little river flashed vividly before her mind. She was longing for a time and a place which were gone for ever and for people she could never see again.

Twenty-Three

Miss Agnes and Miss Laetitia came to say good-bye. Miss Agnes brought the letter which she had received from the Lord Lieutenant's office. She read it aloud to Marya. His Excellency the Lord Lieutenant did not have precise details of Tom's address. The Australian authorities had given tickets of leave to Irish prisoners who were sentenced for stealing food. Tom was free but had to register with the local magistrate of police. He was last known to have registered with the magistrate of police at Moreton Bay.

"Moreton Bay? Is that in Australia, ma'am?" Marya asked. She avoided looking at Miss Gillen. She would probably be scolded again for presuming to speak to visitors but she did not care.

"Yes, it is in Australia," Miss Agnes said. "We looked in the atlas. It is in one of the new territories."

Marya was disappointed. She still had no address for Tom. "Thank you for making the enquiry for me," she said politely.

"But aren't you going to write to your uncle? If you send it care of the magistrate of police at Moreton Bay, he may know where to deliver it."

Marya hesitated. There were still insurmountable difficulties. Would the Board of Guardians allow her to write a letter? Who would pay for postage?

"I've brought you a pencil and paper," Miss Laetitia said, taking the items from a paper bag. "I thought a pencil would be best. I don't suppose you know how to write with a pen."

Marya looked at Miss Gillen. "May I?"

Miss Gillen nodded but looked displeased. Marya sat down at the end of a bench and wrote to Tom. She hoped that he was well. She hoped that Susan and the baby and old Peter were also well. She told that Mama and Packey were dead and that she and Marya were about to set off for Sydney, Australia. She did not know how to spell Sydney, Australia. Rachel whispered the letters to her.

Miss Laetitia folded the letter into an envelope. "May I use your pen and ink, Miss Gillen?" she asked. She sat down at Miss Gillen's table and addressed the letter to Tom Gilbride, care of the Magistrate of Police, Moreton Bay,

Australia. She ornamented her capital letters with beautiful curls and flourishes.

"Thank you, ma'am," Marya said with a polite curtsey.

Miss Laetitia put the envelope into the paper bag and tucked the bag into a deep pocket in her wide skirt. She drew out another paper bag full of sugar lumps and presented one to each girl. Miss Agnes also produced a paper bag and gave each girl what looked like a round white sweet. Marya popped it in her mouth. The taste was horrible. She took it out of her mouth as discreetly as possible and held it in her hand.

"The sugar is to sweeten your voices," Miss Laetitia announced. "The camphor balls are to put in your sea chests to keep moths away. Now, everybody sing!" She waved her arms to mark time while Miss Agnes led the hymn in her shrill quavering voice. Marya sang too, in spite of the vile taste of camphor in her mouth. If only her letter would reach Tom, he might come to Sydney to find them.

As soon as the old ladies left the schoolroom, Miss Gillen turned furiously on Marya. "Such impertinence," she said indignantly. "You had better learn your proper station before you reach Australia. No mistress wants a servant who does not know her place."

Servant: the word took Marya by surprise.

Were they to be servants in Australia? She felt vaguely disappointed. She had imagined that they were setting off to seek their fortunes, not to be hired out as servants. On the other hand, there was a lot to be said for having the security of a position and a home with a good mistress. She would have to think about it.

With overcrowding, fever broke out in the house again. The girls who were to go to Australia anxiously counted the days till their departure, terrified that sickness might keep them from going.

The Master had a relapse of fever. Nobody ever survived a relapse. Now that she knew he would soon be dead, Marya found that her hatred for him evaporated. She felt almost sorry for him.

"I'll never forgive him," Hannah said bitterly. "Dying is too good for him."

The Board did not wait for his demise. They quickly appointed a new Master and also appointed an assistant Master, whose name was Sergeant Healy. It would be Sergeant Healy's duty to escort the orphan girl emigrants to Plymouth.

He was a stout, cheerful man with enormous moustaches. His walk was brisk and erect, probably because he had been a soldier. He spoke with a big, booming voice. When he supervised the men at their labour of breaking stones in the men's yard his voice echoed through the buildings and could be heard in the girls' wing.

The girls packed their newly-made clothes and their second pair of shoes into wooden sea chests which were provided for them. Each girl was given a comb for herself alone, a button-hook for fastening the new boots, sewing needles, thimble and thread for mending and a two-pound block of soap.

Marya and Breege were given back the clothes which they were wearing when they came to the workhouse. Mama and Packey's clothes were in the bundle. When they unrolled them, a small cloth bundle fell out. Marya opened it carefully. It contained the few things that Mama had kept when she gave her other posessions away.

There was a piece of grey flannel which had come from an old shirt of Dada's. The long bone needle which he had used for mending nets was wrapped in the flannel. There was a cross which Mama had woven from rushes. It used to hang on a nail on the back of the door. Marya handled it gently because the rushes were crushed and withered. She put it back into the bundle and laid it among the petticoats. They had no use for the ragged petticoats but they folded them carefully and placed them in their sea chests.

Doctor Kelly examined each girl. He found them all fit to travel. The chaplains wrote references for the girls of their own flock and came in turn to speak to them about the perils which lay ahead. "You will be given into the care of your employers," the Catholic chaplain said. "Be dutiful, honest and truthful and they will deal fairly with you."

He gave out rosaries which Catholic gentlewomen of the town had bought for them. The girls put the rosaries round their necks and knelt while the chaplain said a prayer of blessing over them. They prayed for their relatives who were dead or in foreign lands. Marya felt a strange sense of kinship with those who had left Ireland already, driven by hunger across vast oceans. She thought of Seamus and his comical freckled face and included him in her prayer. Perhaps, by this time, he had been sentenced to transportation. That would mean a ticket of leave for him in Australia. She might even meet him there some day.

On the morning of their departure they put on their new clothes. Marya's dress was of coarse brown linen, made with a full skirt and loose sleeves which were gathered at shoulder and cuff. The coarse material did not rub her skin because underneath it she had on a fine cambric vest, and there were five more cambric vests in her sea chest.

She had a choice of petticoats, one of white linen and one of red flannel. The ward was chilly, so she chose the red petticoat and packed the white one into her sea chest. Her new brown boots came above her ankle and buttoned up the side. Under the boots she wore long woollen stockings which reached above her knee.

She wished she had a mirror to see herself. A long mirror like the one in the Master's rooms. Never before had she worn such fine clothes.

They walked two by two through the town, across the bridge and down the lane to the harbour. A cart laden with their sea chests had gone before them. Curious townspeople came to doors and windows to look at the orphans who were going to Australia. Some young men cheered and wished them luck.

"The blessing of God with you, children," an old white-capped woman called out in Irish from an upstairs window. Marya waved back to show her that she understood.

Twenty-Four

The ship was moored a short distance from the quay. Her name, *The Sarah of Ramsey,* could be read in faded white letters on her bow. They had to line up and wait for their names to be called by a customs officer. Then each girl was inspected by a medical officer.

They were ferried out, eight at a time, and were hoisted on board. When it was Marya's turn to go down the slimy stone steps of the quay she touched the grey limestone of the quay wall, reminding herself that this was the last time she would touch Ireland. She thought of the last time she had gone down those same steps. Mama and Dada and Packey were still alive. Tom and Susan and Peter were with them. A lump came in her throat. She touched the wall once again and stepped into the boat.

Girls who had never been in a boat before screamed in fright each time the boat rocked. They shrieked even more as they were winched on to the ship and swung at the end of a rope above the water. Breege tried to be sedate but started to giggle when Rachel was swinging and screaming hysterically over the water.

"Right, you next," the boatman said grimly. "We'll see if you laugh as much when you're up there."

He looped the rope round Breege who giggled even more at the sight of his dour face. She went on giggling as she was lifted in the air and was laughing hysterically when she was swung on to the deck. Marya was hoisted up next, followed by Hannah. The Sergeant was allowed to climb a rope-ladder which hung over the side.

The boat had an atmosphere of its own. It creaked and rattled. A strong smell of salted fish rose from between the boards of the deck and from the open holds. A small wooden shack sat on deck between the main mast and the bow. "Thon's your quarters," a sailor said, pointing at the shack.

"That?" Sergeant Healy said. "One big wave would carry that thing away."

"Not you, sir, you'll berth in the fo'c'sle. The deck cabin is for female passengers."

The girls went inside the deck cabin and found that it was empty. There was not even straw to lie on. They went back outside to watch the sailors haul anchor and let the ship be towed downstream. When they were almost at the river bar, the sails were hoisted. For an instant the great mainsail hung slack, then filled with wind. The ship moved swiftly across the bar and out to the open sea.

"Look, there's the black rock," Breege said.

Marya watched as they passed the black rock and the dunes. They glimpsed the rocky shore where they had gathered seaweed and shellfish. For an instant the land opened and showed the old mill and the line of willows by the river. Then they vanished from sight.

They sailed north, moving swiftly past a land of high mountains which rose in sheer cliffs from the sea. Darkness fell. The sergeant called them together and a sailor served soup and portions of hard bread. They squatted on deck because there was nowhere to sit. When they finished, they went into the cabin and lay close together for warmth.

They woke early. Chilly draughts came in on all sides of the deck cabin. When they went out on deck they had to hold on to the sides of the deck cabin because the boat was rolling, tacking against an unfavourable wind. It still followed the coast but now the land inched by them, rising and falling with each roll of the boat.

"Breakfast," Sergeant Healy called.

"Not me," Marya said.

"Me neither."

"I don't want anything."

"Are you all seasick?" the sergeant asked sympathetically. "You'd better go inside and lie down again."

The girls went back into the cabin. Marya went outside just once during the morning, to vomit over the side.

"There's the coast of Antrim," the sergeant said.

She didn't bother to look. Spray blew in her face and the sails made ripping noises above her head. The stench of fish was everywhere. She retched and was sick again.

The day was endless. The girls were rocked and rolled about. They tried to stay put in one place but the next roll heaved them about again.

On the third day they recovered from seasickness. They got up and went out on deck. Sergeant Healy brought boiling water from the galley and made tea. He pointed out the Isle of Man and they saw a steam packet belching black smoke on its way to some island port.

There was no sign of land again till they saw the westernmost tip of Cornwall. So that is England, Marya thought. It was not so different. There were rocks and hills just like at home. A fresh westerly wind filled the sails and the ship gathered speed as it entered the Channel. Marya sat on deck, leaning over the side to watch the churning white wake the boat left behind. Within hours they were entering the narrow straits of Plymouth sound.

For two days they were confined on board. The sailor who served their meals brought always the same thing, greasy soup and bread. The bread was hard and the soup consisted of lumps of suet floating in greasy hot water. "Anyone want more of this delicious consomme," Rachel asked. There were no takers, so she emptied it over the side.

On the third day they were ferried to the land and led by Sergeant Healy through the streets of Plymouth to the emigrant depot. The depot was a tall grey building. Inside, it looked a lot like the workhouse with long tables and benches. Sergeant Healy said good-bye and wished them well in their new life.

"You girls, line up," said a brisk little woman. She gave each girl a pewter bowl, a mug and three pieces of cutlery. "Now your bedding. Line up again." They were issued with two sheets each, a blanket and a mattress.

The woman lined them up once more and led them to a long room lined with bunks three deep. "Now, make up your beds for the night. When you hear the bell, bring your utensils and line up at the dining-hall."

There were other girls in the room, who stared curiously at the newcomers. They were well-dressed, with bonnets and new boots. Orphans, like themselves. They did not have time to find out who the strangers were. They had no sooner finished making their beds than the sound of a gong summoned them back to the dining-hall for supper.

Next morning, they walked two by two to the docks. They made a very long line. Marya thought there must be a couple of hundred girls, maybe more. She was glad they didn't have far to walk. She had tied up her mattress and blanket and slung them on her back but they still seemed an enormous weight. When they came to a stop on a wooden wharf, she gratefully put down her load.

The small woman in charge pointed to a huge square-built ship with two tall masts which was anchored a short distance offshore. "That's the ship that will take you to Australia," she said. The ship loomed high above the water. Its sides were tarred black and her name, *Inchinaan*, was painted across her wide bow.

They waited for almost an hour and watched small boats ferrying between the ship and the shore, taking on men and supplies. At last it was their turn. They climbed down from the wharf into the boats and were ferried out, twenty at a time. Once more they were winched up from the small boats, complete with their bundles of bedding, and then set down on the deck. Rachel seemed to have got over her fear of being winched up in the air and did not scream.

There were girls already on board, girls they had not met in the depot. They were raucous and loud. "Up, up, up," they jeered as each girl was winched on board.

"They must think we can't climb ladders," Marya said in disgust as she was dropped unceremoniously on deck.

"Don't complain or they'll make you climb the mast," said one of the jeering girls. Marya was surprised at their appearance. They were different. Perhaps they weren't orphans. They were untidy and their clothes were shabby. They spoke English with oddly musical accents and were free and rowdy in their behaviour. There seemed to be nobody in charge of them.

The remaining girls arrived on deck and clustered in groups according to which workhouse they had come from. Marya spoke to a girl on the edge of a group but she did not seem to understand. She tried Irish and the girl replied, but in a dialect so different to Marya's own that she barely understood the few murmured words of greeting.

"Where do we sleep?" Marya asked but

received no reply. She could see no cabin on deck.

A small boy who wore wide sailor's trousers passed with a bucket of slops. "Where do we sleep?" Breege asked him.

He grinned. "You can share my hammock if you like."

"Hammock?" Breege echoed. "What's a hammock?"

"You girls, no fraternising with the crew," called an angry voice. It belonged to a squat red-faced man. He did not appear to be a sailor. He was dressed like a gentleman with a long coat, satin waistcoat and tall hat. A heavy silver watch chain lay across his waistcoat. "How dare you speak to a sailor! What is your name?"

"Brigid Gilbride. I didn't know it was not allowed."

The man glared fiercely. "The sweepings of Irish workhouses," he muttered with contempt. He darted angry looks about the deck to make sure that no other girl dared to speak to the crew.

"Where are we to sleep, sir?" Marya asked. He seemed to be in charge.

"In the between-decks."

Marya was relieved. There would be no precarious deck cabin this time. Between-decks sounded much more secure. "May we put our baggage down there now, sir?"

"You will do nothing of the sort. Remain where you are till the Matron comes on board."

Marya put her bundle down on the deck and sat on it. An hour passed. Girls wandered forward and back, not quite certain what to do with themselves. How were they to know what they might and might not do? When they walked too far forward the angry man pursued them, puffing with rage. "How dare you girls approach the forecastle. How dare you!"

"What's the forecastle?" someone asked.

"That's the forecastle." The man indicated the high front deck. "Those are the crew's quarters. If I see any of you further forward than the main mast, I will order you to the poop."

Nobody dared to ask what the poop was.

Twenty-Five

During the hours which followed, supplies were loaded on board. Barrels, boxes and bags were hoisted up on deck. Bundles of hay and straw were ferried out and stacked under an awning made of sailcloth. Marya watched in astonishment as a barge carrying a cow, two goats, a pig and a great many chickens in wicker baskets was towed out by two boats. The cow lowed unhappily and the chickens squawked.

The cow was the first animal hoisted on board. It was secured by ropes and led to a pen on the port side of the ship. The chickens and the other animals followed. The pig was penned and the goat tethered. The chickens were left in their wicker baskets.

At last a boat drew alongside, laden with trunks and boxes. In the prow sat a middle-aged woman wrapped in shawls. Her bonnet was ornamented with coloured feathers. Her hand rested on an umbrella which maintained an upright position in spite of the motion of the boat. Opposite her sat a thin pale-faced girl who was also wrapped in shawls.

"Look at this," Rachel said with glee. "It must be the Matron. She'll look well dangling on the end of a rope."

The rope was lowered to the boat. One by one, the items of baggage were hoisted on board while the lady gave precise instructions. The pale girl was winched up on deck and stood motionless while a sailor untied the rope. Then the lady's turn came. She looked disdainfully at the rope which was lowered for her and spoke sharply to one of the boatmen.

"Have you got a chair?" he called up to the sailor at the winch.

A chair was quickly found and lowered. The lady sat stiff-backed on it while the rope was secured. She hovered in the air, a picture of dignity.

"Does she think she's Queen Victoria?" Rachel whispered.

The chair swung for a moment above the deck and was gently lowered. The lady stood up and arranged her skirts. The squat man with the tall hat hurried to her side. He removed his hat and bowed deeply. "I am the surgeon superintendent, your servant, ma'am."

The woman looked past him at the crowd of girls. "So these are the Irish paupers?"

"Yes, ma'am," said the surgeon. "They are all here. The sweepings of Irish workhouses."

"Why are they on deck? Why are they not below?"

"They are awaiting your instructions, ma'am."

The woman turned to the girls. "All of you girls, go below at once. You may not come on deck without permission."

A sailor showed the way. There were two hatches with ladders leading below. The girls climbed down into the between-decks.

The first thing that Marya noticed was the foul smell. "Bilge-water," a sailor said. "You're just above the bilge." It took several minutes to see in the dim light. The ceiling was low, allowing barely enough room to stand upright. Bunks, two deep, were secured against the ship's sides. In the middle, between the lines of bunks, were long tables and benches secured to the floor. Their sea chests were already below, stacked in the empty spaces between the bunks and the tables.

Marya and Breege chose their bunks with Rachel and Hannah alongside. They searched among the sea chests to find their own and carried them to their bunks. There were squabbles among girls who were unable to find a bunk close to their friends. One of the shabby girls flung another girl's bundle out on the floor. The girl who owned the bundle put it back on the bunk and flung the other girl's out. Half a dozen of her friends gathered round.

"All right, all right, I know when I'm outnumbered," the shabby girl said, picking up her bundle and looking around for an empty bunk.

"There's an empty bunk here," Marya said.

The girl reluctantly placed her bundle on a top bunk. She turned fiercely to Marya and said, "You just don't touch anything that's mine and I'll leave your things alone."

"I don't want to touch your things."

"What! Do you think I have a disease or something?"

"No, I didn't mean anything like that."

"That's all right. You just watch it." She turned to Breege and Rachel. "What are you looking at? Have I got horns on me?"

They looked away. The girl spread her mattress and unwrapped her bowl and cutlery from a sheet. Marya stole a look and wondered why she did not have a sea chest. What she was wearing looked like well-worn workhouse clothes.

"What's your name?" she asked.

The girl turned with a fierce air and then relented. "Rosanna." She caught sight of Marya's possessions spread out on her mattress. "What's that?" she asked, pointing at the button-hook.

"It's for fastening the buttons on my boots. My name is Marya."

Rosanna looked closely at Marya's boots, then picked up the hem of her dress. "You've got a flannel petticoat and all. Are you an orphan?"

"Yes. Aren't you?"

"Yes, I'm an orphan. Did you come from a workhouse?"

"Yes."

"You have a wild lot of nice things for orphans." She looked enviously at Marya's spare clothes.

"The Board of Guardians paid for the cloth. We made most of the clothes ourselves."

"Lucky you. Our Guardians are a lot of skinflints. They said they were giving us this and that to get us to go, but all they gave us in the end was the clothes we were standing up in. And they wouldn't have given us those only they couldn't send us out naked."

"They gave us shoes. Don't forget the shoes," a girl shouted from a top bunk across on the other side. She waved a leg with a huge, heavy laced brogue on the end of it. "They got them all made the same size, big so that they would fit everyone."

"It's a good thing that we had an odd stitch of

our own," said Rosanna, tightening a ragged plaid shawl around her. "This shawl was my mother's. They let me take it with me."

"She's Emily," she said, pointing at the other girl. "We used to have our own wages. We worked in the woollen mill till we got laid off. We're used to better than this."

It was almost as if she came from another country, Marya thought. What sort of mill was a woollen mill? She had heard of flour mills and there was the old disused flax mill on the river but mill work was heavy work. Only men worked in a mill.

"This is my sister, Breege. And this is Rachel and Hannah."

"Did you see the cut of the Matron?" Rosanna said with a shriek of amusement. "Lady Muck."

Marya shook her head frantically at her and put a finger on her lips. She could see what Rosanna could not, that Matron had just appeared through a door behind her.

The Matron looked about but did not seem to have heard. "You, you and you," she said pointing at Rosanna, Marya and Breege, "come with me."

They followed her through to her own quarters, a small low-ceilinged cabin with two beds which were merely bunks fastened to the floor. "Go up on deck and fetch my baggage."

Twenty-Six

There was a separate ladder leading from a small space outside the cabin door. The girls climbed up and emerged again on the deck. The Matron followed. The pale girl was sitting on a trunk but stood up to let Marya and Rosanna take it.

"Careful with that trunk," the Matron warned. "I have medicines in it."

Rosanna and Marya took the trunk between them and lowered it down the companionway. Breege followed with two large bags. Behind her came the pale girl. Last to descend was the Matron, holding up her voluminous skirts with one hand and clinging to the ladder with the other. The pale girl watched listlessly as Matron unlocked the trunk and raised the lid.

Out of it came pillows, sheets and feather quilts. She piled bedding into Marya's arms. Marya felt the softness of the quilts and wondered did all of the better classes sleep in such luxury.

"You, girl, arrange these beds," the Matron said. "You, too," she pointed at Breege. The girls spread the sheets and then the quilts. Marya looked dubiously at the pillows and pillowcases. "You put the pillows into the pillowcases," the Matron said sharply. "Haven't you ever made a bed before?"

Marya felt angry. She would have liked to shout at the Matron, to say "no, I have never seen a bed made up with pillows and sheets" but she held her tongue. People who had knew nothing about people who hadn't. She suddenly remembered that she had once seen a bed with pillows and a quilt, in the Master's quarters. That was not something she wanted to remember.

She stuffed a pillow into a pillowcase and looked to see what Rachel was doing. Rachel was watching to see what she was doing. They shrugged in amusement. The Matron made no further comment. She was busy unwrapping layers of shawls from around the pale girl.

"Now, Eliza, you must lie down and sleep for a little while."

"I don't need to sleep, Mamma," Eliza protested.

"Nonsense, of course you do."

Eliza let her mother remove her shoes and lay down on the feather quilt. The bed was narrow, barely eighteen inches wide. The Matron's bed was the same. Marya wondered how the portly Matron would make herself comfortable in such a narrow space.

When they went back to the between-decks, supper had arrived. A pot of gruel had been lowered through a hatch. The Matron ladled gruel into bowls and poured milk from an enormous jug. So that was what the cow was for, Marya thought. Fresh milk on board.

She carried her bowl and mug back to the table nearest her bunk and took her knife, fork and spoon out of a deep pocket in her skirt. The knife and the spoon she understood, but what was the purpose of the fork? The only fork she had ever seen was a lot bigger than this. It was used in the potato gardens for lifting manure or in the workhouse for cleaning latrines.

"What's it for?" she asked Rosanna.

"It's for putting the food into your mouth. You country girls have never seen nothing, have you?"

"What's wrong with fingers?"

"Forks is more genteel."

Marya tried lifting gruel with the fork. "It doesn't work, does it?"

"No, you only use a fork for things you would eat with your fingers."

"Even bread?"

"No, not bread. You can eat that with your fingers."

It all sounded very complicated.

After supper, they went in turn to rinse the bowls and spoons. Matron rapped the table and announced, "Everyone to bed now."

There was a chorus of objections. "On board ship, you go to bed at eight o'clock. Now it is time for bed." She read a prayer and allowed a few minutes for undressing. Then she turned down the lamps and locked the door which led to her own cabin. A few minutes later, Marya heard the sound of gratings being secured over the hatches. They were locked in.

She lay in her bunk thinking of the incredible journey which lay ahead. For four months, they would be locked for endless hours in this dark space between-decks. From Matron's cabin she could hear persistent coughing. It sounded like Eliza. Perhaps she was sick. That would explain why she wore so many shawls.

Far below there was the sound of bilge-water slushing to and fro. The motion of the boat stirred up the water and made the foul smell stronger. Her bunk tilted forward and back, then forward again. We must be under way, she thought. Four months of stink. Maybe we'll get used to it.

In the morning they were up and dressed before Matron came in. The hatches were opened and daylight lit up the spaces below the hatches.

The Matron sorted them into what she called messes, each mess being the number of girls who could sit round a table. Then she allocated work to each table, their days for scrubbing floors and for cleaning the privies and baths which were in small partitioned rooms at the front end of the between-decks.

"You have an hour on deck to collect your rations and have breakfast. When you hear the bell, you will come back down here to do your chores."

They climbed up on deck, blinking in the bright light of day. The ship was cutting through the water at speed. A fresh breeze roared in the sails and sailors shouted to one another high up in the rigging. The cabin boy perched on top of the forecastle and whistled at the girls as they lined up for their day's food and water allowance.

"I'm the second mate," announced the seaman who seemed to be in charge of their rations. He called the cabin boy to him and boxed his ears. Then he turned to the girls once more. "Don't eat all your rations at once. There will be no more till tomorrow. Water is for drinking only. Any washing of clothes or bedding must be done on deck with seawater. Buckets are provided for drawing water over the side."

The portions of food seemed lavish. There was hard biscuit, a large piece of bread, oatmeal, raisins, sugar, cocoa and a piece of dried salt meat for each girl. Milk was poured into each mug. Each mess was apportioned a small keg of drinking water which was to last all day.

Matron led the girls forward and showed them the galley where they could cook their rations. Beside the galley was a condenser, an ingenious machine which could turn salt water into fresh. Matron took charge of the rations of oatmeal and supervised the cooking of it for breakfast. Marya ate her share of porridge hungrily. She examined the raisins in her rations and gingerly tasted one. It was sweet, so sweet that she ate all the raisins at once, keeping none for later. It hardly mattered. She still had lots of food, biscuits, bread, cocoa and meat.

She spent the remainder of the hour on deck wandering about with Breege, Rachel and Hannah. They went to look at the animals in their pens and the chickens in their baskets. Rosanna and Emily did not join them. With their unsuitable clothing, they were too cold to stay on deck for long.

The deck was surrounded by a wooden rail. Marya leaned on it, watching the frothing wake behind. There was no sign of land anywhere.

When the bell rang, they went back down to tidy and clean the between-decks. The Matron inspected the bunks to see that they were tidy. She summoned the ship's carpenter and ordered him to add an extra board to her bunk since it was much too narrow for a grown woman.

The girls took turns carrying down seawater. They scrubbed and cleaned till the wooden floor was white. It was slow to dry. Not enough air for drying entered through the open hatches. The Matron gave instructions to a sailor to stretch pieces of sailcloth at an angle over the hatches to create a draught below.

"Ma'am, this is a ship, not a dolls' house," protested the second mate.

The Matron drew herself up indignantly. "I beg your pardon?" The second mate withdrew, muttering that a ship was no place for women. However, the awnings were put in place.

The girls looked at the Matron with new respect. The mate was a person of importance. He wore a uniform with bright buttons and a cap with a shiny peak. Yet Matron ordered him about as if he were a servant.

Twenty-Seven

When all was cleaned below she inspected each girl's luggage to see that everyone was properly supplied. When she came to Rosanna she was dismayed. "Where are your shifts and warm clothing?"

"I don't have any."

"You don't have any? What happened to them?"

"We weren't given any."

"None of you?"

"No, ma'am."

"Then you will have to make them."

She had come prepared. Two bolts, one of red flannel and one of brown worsted cloth, appeared from a trunk along with a pair of giant shears. She stretched the material on the clean floor and cut out pieces for dresses and petticoats. Then she gave a bundle of pieces to each of the girls who needed them.

"What will I do with these, ma'am?" Rosanna asked in dismay.

"Can't you sew?"

"No, ma'am."

Matron inspected the dresses worn by the girls who were properly provided. "You made this yourself?" she asked when she came to Breege.

"Yes, ma'am."

"Then you take two of these girls and show them how to sew the pieces together."

Marya was also chosen to instruct two girls. They sat in the gangway between the bunks, under the light of the swaying lamps and stitched the pieces of cloth together. Rosanna's sewing was hopeless. She tried clumsily to thread a needle. Marya took it and threaded it. Then she set Rosanna to do simple tacking. She managed to tack two pieces together and whooped with delight. She worked eagerly then, sure that she could master the business of sewing eventually.

Matron distributed hanks of wool and knitting-needles to those of the remaining girls who knew how to knit and set them to work knitting stockings. The leftover flannel was set aside for making warm shifts. "There will be cold weather before we reach Australia," Matron said. "You will need all your warm clothing."

At dinner-time they stopped sewing. Marya gnawed her piece of dried meat. It tasted disgusting. Some of the girls brought drinking water to the galley, boiled it and dipped the dried meat into the hot water. It didn't improve it. After chewing on it for a while, Marya got used to the taste. She ate some bread as well and kept what was left for later.

In the afternoon they walked on deck again. Eliza was on deck already, wrapped in shawls and sitting on a chair. She looked lonely and bored. Marya would have liked to talk to her but was afraid of offending. They did not stay very long on deck. The breeze was cold and soon drove them below.

The days flew by. Sewing and knitting passed the time. Marya sang softly while she worked and Breege joined in. They sang one of Mama's old airs.

The door which led to the cabin opened and Eliza came in. She sat down on a form and listened. When the song ended she asked, "Do you know any more songs?"

Breege nodded and started to sing again. This time Marya took up the descant. Eliza sat perfectly still, as though in a trance. When the second song ended she rose and went out as silently as she had come.

In a short while she came back with a book in her hand. "Would you like me to read to you?"

"Yes, please do," voices chorused from around the room.

She read slowly, in a clear voice, a tale of knights and beautiful maidens. The story lasted for almost an hour. The girls listened in rapt silence. When the story ended Eliza closed her book and rose. "I'll read for you again tomorrow, if you like."

The next day nobody cared about hearing stories. The boat pitched and rolled. Water crashed against the sides and, when a wave washed over the deck, salt water poured down through the spaces around the hatches.

Marya thought she would die. "It is only *mal de mer*," said the Matron, holding on to the fixed tables to make her way down the room. She retreated again to her own bunk, leaving the door open. It swung to and fro with each lurch of the boat.

"Is it the fever?" Rosanna wailed. "What did she call it?"

"I don't know what she called it but I think it's just seasickness. We had it on the way to Plymouth."

"Sick as dogs," Rachel agreed. She retched suddenly and vomited over the side of her bunk.

"I have sent for the surgeon," Matron announced on the second day of the storm. "He might be able to do something." She reeled back to her cabin, shutting the door this time.

The surgeon did not appear. The second mate came to report that the surgeon superintendent was confined to his cabin by seasickness. "We're just coming into the Bay of Biscay," he said cheerfully, holding on to the door jambs for support. "We'll be back in calm waters in five or six days." The girls moaned.

It was not as bad as the mate promised. It took only four days of nausea to reach calm waters again. The between-decks was filthy. Girls on higher bunks had been sick over lower bunks. The floor was slippery with filth. Hardly anybody had made it to the privies and, besides, the privies had overflowed with the motion of the boat.

The hatches were opened and sunlight shone into the darkness. They went out on deck and breathed clean air. The air was warm, like summer. Marya thought Matron must have been mistaken about cold weather ahead. The sun shone from a clear blue sky. The ship barely moved, its wake reduced to a ripple.

They had bread and milk for breakfast. Then came the cleaning-up. They dragged mattresses and blankets up on deck, washed them and spread them out to dry. The cabin boy slung ropes as clothes lines for them to hang out sheets and clothing. He stayed to haul up a bucket of water for Breege.

"Have you got a sweetheart?" he asked.

"No, I don't," she said suspiciously. The cabin boy was undersized, about as high as her shoulder. She snatched the bucket of water from him and carried it below.

They scrubbed the floor of the between-decks and washed out the privies. When all was clean they lined up again for rations. The rations were abundant; five days food in one. Marya feasted on raisins till she began to feel sick again. She put her portion of meal into the common pot and had gruel for dinner and supper.

Twenty-Eight

The weather grew warmer day by day. Once, in the evening, they saw islands to the west. Lit by the setting sun, they looked like a vision of heaven.

Miss Eliza was on deck. "What are those islands, ma'am?" Marya asked.

"Those are the Canary Islands."

Marya felt envious. She wished she could know things, like Miss Eliza. But she wouldn't like to be so pale and so thin.

The weather grew hotter. Even when there was a breeze, the air was heavy with heat. They sat on deck wearing their lightest dresses and their straw hats. Matron set the girls who did not have hats to sew cotton bonnets. Rosanna was delighted with her bonnet. In spite of the heat, she found energy to walk up and down the deck to let one particular brown-eyed sailor see how she looked in it.

Night-time was even worse. The between-decks was stifling but the surgeon superintendent still insisted on locking the gratings over the hatches at night. It was hard to believe that it was December.

On Christmas Day there was an extra ration of raisins. They sat on deck and sang Christmas carols while the sun blazed down.

"I'm engaged to be married," Rosanna whispered to Marya. "His name's John."

"You'll get caught."

"I don't care. I love him and he loves me."

They crossed the line next day. "The line is the equator," Miss Eliza explained to Marya. "It's exactly halfway between north and south."

There really wasn't a line, Marya realised. Except on maps.

The sailors were allowed to stop work and were given a double ration of rum. A sailor played hornpipes on a fiddle and tipsy sailors stamped their feet and danced on top of the forecastle. The cabin boy was tied to the end of a rope and ducked in the ocean because it was his first time to cross the line.

Some girls began to dance with each other, on their side of the deck. Where was Rosanna? Marya wondered. She couldn't see her anywhere.

Suddenly there was angry shouting from the galley and she knew that Rosanna was caught. "To the poop, girl, to the poop," the surgeon superintended raged, dragging Rosanna along the deck. He flung her down in front of Matron.

Matron was imperturbable. "Well, girl, what have you been up to?"

"What has she been up to? I'll tell you what she has been up to. Fraternising!"

"Is this true?" Matron asked.

"I'm engaged to him, ma'am," Rosanna explained. "We're going to be married."

"To the poop," the doctor shouted.

"Yes, I'm afraid it must be the poop," Matron agreed.

The doctor dragged Rosanna away by the arm. He led her to the rear of the boat and up a ladder to the poop deck at the very back of the ship. "Now, girl, you will stay there for a full hour. That will give you time to repent of your disgraceful behaviour." He turned and descended to the main deck. "One hour, one full hour," he said in a terrible voice, "not a minute less."

Marya watched in amazement. That was it? The terrible punishment? She wanted to laugh but did not dare for fear of enraging the doctor further.

It was not entirely the end of the matter. On Sunday morning when the doctor read them a sermon, he paused at the end of his reading to ask them to pray for an unrepentant sinner in their midst. The sinner had erred again and had been caught again. He would not put her on the poop deck on the Sabbath but tomorrow she would be punished. She would spend two hours on the poop deck.

"I feel it my duty to warn you of the consequences of bad behaviour on this ship. Anyone whose conduct is not as it should be will not be permitted to land at Sydney. She will be sent north to Moreton Bay."

Moreton Bay! Marya could hardly believe her ears. Where Tom was registered with the magistrate of police. All she had to do was misbehave.

She talked it over with Breege. "We have to do something really bad."

"I'll steal sugar from the galley."

"Remember, you have to get caught."

"I'll get caught."

In the morning Breege stole a cup of sugar. Nothing happened. "I'll take a bowl of sugar tomorrow," she promised.

"We want to go to Moreton Bay, me and Breege," Marya said to Rosanna.

"You're mad. The surgeon says it's practically a wilderness."

"Yes, but my uncle is there."

"Why don't you just ask to be sent there?"

"They mean to hire us out as servants in Sydney. They might not let us go to Moreton Bay."

"So you're going to be bad like me?"

"Yes, and you can help me."

When the doctor came for Rosanna. She resisted being brought to the poop. "Help, I don't want to," she shrieked as she was dragged along.

"You brute," Marya shouted at the doctor. "Let her alone, you bully." She seized Rosanna's other arm and tried to pull her away from the doctor.

"So, there are two of you, are there?" The doctor seized Marya and dragged the two girls, struggling and screaming, to the poop. The second mate had to help the doctor drag them up the ladder.

"Now, you will both stay there for two hours. Not a minute less."

"No, I won't," Marya screamed. She flung herself down on the poop deck and hammered it with her fists. "I won't, I won't."

They stayed for two hours on the poop. The doctor had told them that they must stand, so they lay down and watched the wake of the ship making white waves below them.

"Do you think that was enough to get me to Moreton Bay?"

"It should be. You can do it when I get caught again. That way you'll be sure."

Matron called Marya to her cabin when she came down from the poop. "I'm concerned about you," she said. "Do you often have hysterical attacks?"

"What?"

"Hysteria. The way you behaved with the doctor. I have asked him not to mention it in your report. It could be the heat, you know. Make sure you drink water often."

Hysteria, Marya repeated to herself when she was allowed to go. "They think it's hysteria," she said to Rosanna.

"What?"

"Hysteria. I'm not responsible for my behaviour. It's the heat."

"You'll have to think of something else."

"You take the sugar, I'll take the biscuit," Marya said to Breege in the morning. There was half a sack of biscuit. It wasn't easy to steal it. She had to lumber across the deck from the galley to the hatch with it bulging under her skirt.

Down in the between-deck she gave it out freely to anyone who wanted it. "Eat it now, before they miss it," she said. It was a bit stale but not too bad.

It wasn't missed for quite a while. At Marya's table, they had eaten Breege's bowl of sugar as well as the stolen biscuit and were feeling quite unwell when the second mate summoned them up on deck.

He looked grim. "Someone has stolen a bag of mouldy biscuit which was meant for the pig. All rations will be cancelled till the person who stole it comes forward."

"It was me," Marya said.

"Where is the biscuit now?"

There was a long silence. Girls glared at Marya. She could imagine how they felt. It was bad enough to have eaten the pig's mouldy biscuit without getting blamed for it.

"I ate it, sir."

"Wait here." He sent a sailor to fetch the Matron and the doctor. The girls stood under the hot sun till they came.

"You again," said the doctor.

"Don't be too hard on her," the Matron said, "you know that she is highly-strung."

"She says she ate half a hundredweight of biscuit," said the second mate.

"My goodness," said the doctor. "Were you hungry?"

"Yes, sir."

"Amazing." He turned to Matron. "Do you think the rations are adequate?"

"Yes, I believe they are."

"Yet she ate four stone of mouldy biscuit. Remarkable. I've never heard of anything like it. Put out your tongue, girl."

Marya showed her tongue.

"Any headache? Any swelling of the hands or feet?"

"No, sir. I just wanted to eat them." Couldn't they see that she was bad? Why were they making excuses for her?

The doctor turned to the Matron. "Keep her under observation. This could be serious."

Twenty-Nine

The Matron led her below deck and insisted that she spend the rest of the day in bed. She checked at intervals to see if her hands or feet were swelling. Miss Eliza came to read to her.

Miss Eliza had grown thinner during the weeks of the voyage. When it was very hot she sat listlessly on deck, almost too weak to move. It was less hot now. Marya felt ashamed of her deceit.

"It's kind of you to read to me but I'm not really sick," she tried to explain.

"The doctor thinks you are."

"There's nothing wrong with me. I'm just bad."

"Oh, no, don't say that. You are all good girls. And so healthy and strong. You can look forward to a wonderful future."

"I hear you coughing at night. Are you sick?"

"I'll be better when we reach Australia. The climate of New South Wales is said to be healthy."

"I hope you get better."

"I will."

She read the same story again, about the knight and the princess. Her eyes were bright and her cheeks were flushed. Sometimes she paused for a moment to catch her breath. Before she reached the end of the story, she had an attack of coughing and held a handkerchief to her mouth. When the attack passed, she lay back in her chair panting for breath.

Marya jumped out of her bunk and ran to Matron's cabin. "Come quickly. Miss Eliza is fainting," she said and dashed back to help. Eliza's handkerchief had dropped on the floor. Marya picked it up and saw that it was stained with blood. She helped Matron bring Eliza to her cabin and lay her on her bed.

Next day Rosanna was caught again. The second mate promised the doctor that he would speak to the sailor and Rosanna spent three hours on the poop. The doctor gave orders for Marya to be kept below so that she would not have hysterics again.

Breege went on stealing sugar. Nobody noticed. She stole some while the second mate was inspecting the galley and he paid no attention.

However, the cabin boy noticed. He had a trick of following Breege about, offering himself to her as a sweetheart. Whenever he spoke to her, she drew herself up to her full height and looked down at him before flouncing away. "Hey, sweetheart, you'll get worms eating all that sugar," he said.

"That's none of your business."

"It isn't good for you."

"I don't eat it. I use it to starch the Matron's petticoats."

"I don't believe you."

"Suit yourself."

"Have you ever been kissed?"

"No."

"Well, you're going to be now." He pounced on her, seized her by the waist and stood on tiptoe with puckered lips. Breege squealed and dropped the bowl of sugar.

"Fraternising," bellowed the doctor. He came at a trot, his face red with rage. "You, boy, report to the second mate. And you, miss, to the poop." He noticed the sugar spilled on the deck and picked up the bowl. "Is this yours?"

"Yes, sir."

"Where did you get this sugar?"

"In the galley."

"To the poop and no more sugar ration for you."

Week by week the air grew temperate, then cold. They ran into heavy seas and strong westerly winds. Marya remembered old Marya in the workhouse who read her hand. "The west wind will blow, and you will cross water." How strange that she could foretell that. The ship raced before the wind, pitching and tossing on gigantic swells.

The girls remained below deck. They occupied themselves with sewing and sometimes Matron read to them. Miss Eliza did not read to them any more. Since the weather had grown colder, she stayed in bed. Marya could hear her coughing at night.

The storms raged for weeks. They grew accustomed to the roaring wind and the shock of waves against the sides of the ship. Sometimes, when the hatches were opened, they saw lightning flashes and heard the roar of thunder above the wind and the sea. When the storms grew worse they carried the baths from the bathrooms and kept them under the closed hatches to catch the water which came in when waves broke over the deck. The milk ration was stopped because the cow and the goat were washed overboard.

Each day when Marya went to tidy Matron's cabin she sang for Eliza, softly in case she was sleeping. Eliza did not stir. One night the doctor was summoned urgently. He stayed in the cabin for a long time.

Next morning, Marya went to the cabin again. Matron was sitting by Eliza's bed. Eliza lay still and pale as death. "Don't bother tidying today," Matron said in a whisper. Marya withdrew and closed the door quietly.

That night, the doctor was called. Morning came and Matron did not appear. The girls went about their duties silently. It was mid-morning when the doctor came out of Matron's cabin.

He called the girls together and spoke quietly to them. "I am sorry to have to tell you that Miss Eliza has passed away. There will be a funeral service this afternoon. Matron will be pleased if you will attend."

A deep gloom settled over the between-decks. Girls talked in whispers and moved about quietly. After dinner, the girls put on their warmest clothes and went up on deck. The doctor read a short sermon and the captain, whom they saw for the first time, read prayers for the dead. Eliza's body was slipped over the side. Matron, veiled in black, went back to her cabin.

Thirty

Rosanna and Breege were put on the poop again. When they came back below they were blue with cold.

"We saw an iceberg," Rosanna said, her teeth chattering. "A big dirty lump of ice, floating on the sea."

"It creaked like old timber," Breege said.

"You're making it up."

"No, we really did."

"Sometimes I wonder if love is worth it," Rosanna said, pulling her blanket round her.

"The cabin boy wants to marry me," Breege said. "I suppose I'll have to tell him sometime that we're too young. I'll be quite sorry to have to break his heart. The doctor was really wild this time. We're sure to be sent to Moreton Bay."

Marya could not bring herself to deceive Matron again. After two days of mourning, Matron had resumed her duties. Sometimes she was red-eyed and looked tired. Marya wondered if she had emigrated for her daughter's sake. If that was so, she had no reason at all now for going to Australia.

Matron still remembered to check Marya's hands and feet each day to make sure there was no swelling. Marya felt ashamed. "There's nothing wrong with me," she insisted.

"Yes, but we must make sure."

"No, you don't understand. There really isn't." It all came out then. She explained that she wanted to be sent to Moreton Bay. Only her bad behaviour wasn't bad enough.

"It is a very primitive colony. Without the comforts of civilisation. I don't think you'd like it at all."

"Yes, but my uncle is there."

"Why on earth didn't you say so? I'll speak to the doctor."

Two weeks later, land was sighted. The sailors cheered and the girls rushed up on deck to see Australia. They still had a long way to go, all the way round the south of the continent to the eastern coast. A breeze off the land carried the scent of flowers. Marya remembered Miss Gillen's lesson. It was summertime in Australia. The flowers would be in bloom.

They busied themselves with washing and mending. The food ration was mouldy and insufficient but nobody complained. It was only to be expected after four months at sea.

Matron took Marya aside. "I have spoken to the doctor. He agrees that in view of your bad behaviour you must be sent north to Moreton Bay." She sounded grave. "The doctor will want to talk to you himself. It might be best if you don't mention your uncle to him."

"He doesn't know that we want to go there?"

"No."

"I see."

The doctor sent for Rosanna and Marya and Breege. He spoke to them at length about the error of their ways. He spoke to Marya in particular. "Do you repent?" he asked.

The girls hesitated. If they repented, they might be allowed to land at Sydney. "Not really," Marya said. "I don't feel as sorry as I ought."

"Me neither," said Breege.

"Rosanna has repented," Marya said. "She has broken off her engagement. Haven't you?"

Rosanna nodded and tried to look repentant.

"Let us give thanks for one soul saved," the doctor intoned solemnly. "And let us pray for the sinners," he added, letting his eyes rest sternly on Marya and Breege.

Thirty-One

They lay at anchor off Sydney for five days. The girls could not be allowed ashore until the emigrant depot was ready to receive them. On the fifth day the ship's surgeon announced that they were to go ashore next morning. All except Breege and Marya. Arrangements would be made to send them to Moreton Bay.

On their last night between decks the girls were too excited to sleep. They packed and unpacked their sea chests. They crowded three or four into a bunk so that they could talk together. Breege and Marya climbed into Rachel's bunk. Hannah was there already. Marya suddenly felt desperately lonely at the prospect of being separated from her friends.

"Maybe some time we'll come to Moreton and visit you," Hannah said.

"Or you might come to Sydney to visit us," Rachel said.

Marya felt tears brimming in her eyes. "It

might be years before we meet again. Maybe never."

"We can write to each other. You write to us at the emigrant depot. They'll know there where we are," Hannah said.

"We will," Breege promised.

"What about me?" Rosanna exclaimed, swinging herself across from her own bunk and squeezing into Rachel's. "What about me, will you write to me?"

"Yes, we will," Marya promised.

"Well, move over now and give me room," Rosanna said, pushing and prodding till she made herself comfortable.

In the morning they said good-bye. Breege and Marya watched as the girls were ferried ashore. Beyond was a city and a lush green land. Green, yet not at all like Ireland.

Matron was the last to leave. She gave Marya two letters. One was addressed to the magistrate of police in Moreton Bay. The second was addressed to the ship's surgeon, the barque *Louisa*. "When you go on board the ship for Brisbane, give these letters to the surgeon. I have written to let the magistrate of police know that you have relatives in Moreton Bay and I have asked the doctor to deliver my letter to him."

She gave Marya a small piece of paper with an address written on it. "Write to me. Tell me how you get on. I know . . . " her voice faltered. "I know that you used to sing for Eliza."

She sat on a chair once more and was lowered into the boat below. Marya waved till she saw her reach the long wooden wharf.

Now there was only herself and Breege. What if they were mistaken? What if there was no one they knew at Moreton Bay? What then?

They stayed on board for another two days. Then they were ferried to the barque *Louisa* which was going north. The ship's surgeon of the *Louisa* took charge of them. He seemed dismayed at having to take them on board. No doubt the surgeon of the *Inchinaan* had warned him that he would be dealing with incorrigible young females.

He was a thin sunburned man with sad blue eyes and a long drooping moustache. "I will have to confine you to your cabin. For your own protection, you understand," he said.

Marya gave Matron's letters to him. He opened the letter which was addressed to himself. "You have relatives in the colony?"

"An uncle."

He seemed relieved. "Very good, very good. Nevertheless, you must remain in your cabin. It is the best thing for you. You will be entering dangerous waters, you know."

"Dangerous?"

"Sharks. Pirates. Natives. That sort of thing."

Pirates? Marya wondered if he was trying to frighten them into staying in their cabin, or were they really venturing on a voyage into the unknown? The surgeon closed the cabin door and a key clicked in the lock. He was not going to trust them very far.

Once a day they were allowed to walk on deck for half an hour. A south wind filled the sails and the ship moved swiftly northward. Marya thought again of old Marya who had read her hand. The south wind, she promised, would bring happiness and friends she had never thought to see again. Perhaps. Now that she was responsible for herself and Breege, she was in deep dread of being disappointed.

Day by day they looked west and saw the new continent unfold. Sometimes they were close enough to land to see a line of white surf where the Pacific crashed on the shore. The lush green of the south gave way to a strange red landscape. The air grew hot and their cabin, below deck, was stifling. Time passed slowly, broken only by the intervals of eating and sleeping. The clang of the ship's bell marked the endless empty hours.

After fourteen days they arrived at Moreton Bay. When they were allowed on deck, the ship was already in the bay and steering into the Brisbane River. Dazzling sunlight shone on deep blue water. In the distance they could see a sprawling town of wooden houses, houses perched high above the ground on timber supports. The river seemed to lead right into the heart of the town. They could see people milling about on the wharves and in the adjoining streets.

Marya felt sick with anxiety. How could she have known that there would so many people? Whatever made her think that she would find one Irish convict among so many?

"You will remain on board until I have notified the magistrate of police that you are here," the doctor said. He ordered Marya and Breege back to their cabin and locked the door. They waited all day. When they heard a key turn in the lock they rose expectantly, but it was only a sailor bringing food and water. He went out without speaking and locked the door again.

All night they waited, too uneasy to sleep. What was keeping the doctor? Why had he not come back for them?

Towards morning they dozed uneasily, still fully dressed. A knock at the door roused them. It was the doctor at last. "Bring your baggage. The magistrate of police has given permission for you to go ashore."

The magistrate of police. Marya wondered desperately whether she had made a mistake.

Why had she been so certain that Tom would be here?

They went up on deck. It was early morning. The sky was pale and the town lay silent and still. Sailors were already lowering their sea chests into a boat. A sailor offered to loop the rope round Marya but she refused. "I can climb down the ladder," she said.

"So can I," said Breege.

They descended the rope-ladder. "Careful, careful," the ship's surgeon said anxiously when the boat rocked. He stood on deck watching as they pulled away and skimmed across the river. Marya turned and looked towards the town. In the pale morning light it looked a strange, alien place. Despair gripped her heart.

How could a solitary letter find its way across the world to this place? And even if it did, how would Tom know that they were here now? Unless . . . she hardly dared to hope. Unless the magistrate of police let him know.

She saw that there were people on the wharf. As they drew closer, she heard voices calling. Calling her name, calling both their names, Marya and Breege. The boat rocked dangerously. Breege was on her feet, shouting and waving.

"Sit down, girl," the boatman shouted.

Breege paid no attention. "Tom, Susan, Peter!" she called.

For an instant Marya saw them clearly. Then everything was blurred. But she had seen that Tom was there on the wharf, and Susan, with a child in her arms. And that old man with white hair, was it not Peter?

The boat swept alongside the wharf. Tom reached down and lifted each of them from the boat. Frantically they kissed and hugged. Old Peter stood quietly, waiting till they had kissed Tom and Susan and the child in Susan's arms. "So you're here at last," he said, taking Marya and Breege each by the hand. He held their hands for a long time, held them tightly, as if he would never let go.

"We'll take you home," Tom said, lifting their sea chests on to a cart.

Home, Marya thought happily. They had come thousands of miles across the world and now, at last, they were going home.